HELP!
I'M TRAPPED IN
THE PRESIDENT'S BODY

HELP!
I'M TRAPPED IN
THE PRESIDENT'S BODY

TODD STRASSER

AN
APPLE
PAPERBACK

SCHOLASTIC INC.
New York Toronto London Auckland Sydney

ISBN 0-590-92166-5

Copyright © 1996 by Todd Strasser.
All rights reserved. Published by Scholastic Inc.
APPLE PAPERBACKS and the APPLE PAPERBACKS logo are registered trademarks of Scholastic Inc.

12 11 10 9 8 7 6   9/9 0 1/0

Printed in the U.S.A.   40

First Scholastic printing, October 1996

To Spencer, Justin, and Jamie Merolla

HELP!
I'M TRAPPED IN
THE PRESIDENT'S BODY

1

"The President's coming tomorrow," said Amanda Gluck. She was standing behind my friend Josh Hopka. Josh was sitting with Andy Kent and me at our regular lunch table in the cafeteria.

"Anyone can blow a spit bubble," Josh said, ignoring Amanda. It was the end of lunch and we were waiting for the bell to ring.

"Yeah, Jake," Andy agreed. "That doesn't rate."

"Chill, guys," I said. "*Blowing* the bubble's only *half* of it. Watch."

I rolled my tongue around in my mouth until I produced a good-size spit bubble. Then I tilted my head back and blew the bubble up into the air. The bubble hovered above me for a second and then started to drift down. *That's* when I drew in a big breath and sucked the bubble back in.

"Ta da!" I grinned.

Josh and Andy looked at each other and nodded reluctantly.

"Okay, that rates," Josh allowed.

"Your turn," I said to Andy.

"Didn't you hear me?" Amanda adjusted her glasses. "I said the President *of the United States* is coming here tomorrow."

Amanda is this skinny girl who wears Coke-bottle glasses with thick green frames, and white blouses with round collars buttoned all the way up.

"Back off, Amanda," Andy said as he ripped the paper off the ends of two straws. "This is important."

Andy dipped the other ends in catsup. Then he leaned back and stuck the bare end of one straw in each nostril.

"Okay," he announced. "On the count of three both straw covers hit the ceiling. *One* . . ."

Josh poured some pepper into his hand.

"*Two* . . ."

Josh blew a pepper cloud into Andy's face.

"*Three* . . . *Ah-chooo!*" Andy lurched forward and sneezed. The catsup-tipped straw covers rocketed over Josh's head and . . . *splat!* . . . hit Amanda right in the eyeglasses.

"Eew! Gross!" a bunch of kids screamed.

"*Ah-chooo!*" Andy sneezed again, then shook his fist at Josh. "You jerk! Why'd you do that?"

"Do what?" Josh asked innocently.

2

"*I'm telling Principal Blanco!*" cried Amanda, who looked like a giant insect with two white antennae hanging off her head.

We watched her run out of the cafeteria.

"What'd she want, anyway?" Andy asked.

"I don't know." Josh shrugged. "Something about the President of the United States."

2

The bell rang and we went to social studies. Our teacher, Ms. Rogers, has wavy black hair, and her eyes are big and blue. She was wearing a blue-and-white striped sweater and blue slacks.

"I have very exciting news." Ms. Rogers's cheeks were flushed with excitement. "The President of the United States is coming."

The class went silent for a moment. Then Josh said, "So?"

"He's coming *here*," Ms. Rogers explained. "To Jeffersonville. To *this* school!"

Julia Saks raised her hand. She is blonde and pretty and always says exactly what's on her mind.

"Yes, Julia?" Ms. Rogers called on her.

"Are you feeling okay?" Julia asked.

The class twittered.

"Well, I'm feeling very excited," Ms. Rogers replied. "Imagine meeting the President."

I raised my hand.

"Yes, Jake?"

"Why is he coming to *this* school?"

"Because the presidential election is next Tuesday," Ms. Rogers explained. "Our state is crucial to the election and the most recent polls show that the voters here are still undecided. All three presidential candidates will be campaigning in this area over the weekend. Then on Monday night they'll have the final presidential debate. And it's going to be held in *our* high school auditorium."

The class exchanged puzzled looks. All three presidential candidates were coming to Jeffersonville High?

Andy raised his hand. "But why is President Frimp even bothering? He doesn't have a chance, does he?"

Clifton Frimp had been President of the United States for almost four years. Nobody had anything good to say about him.

"He is behind in the polls in many states," Ms. Rogers said. "But there's still time to change people's minds. Polls don't mean anything until the votes are counted."

"Isn't he the one who misspelled tomato in that spelling bee?" asked Amber Sweeny.

"Yes," said Ms. Rogers. "But in his defense, this has been an extremely hard fought and grueling campaign for all the candidates. I've read that President Frimp is on the verge of exhaustion.

5

It's not easy to spell everything right when you're exhausted."

"I could understand messing up on embarrass or accommodate," said Josh. "But what kind of mutant misspells tomato?"

The class chuckled. But to me, it wasn't funny. My mom is a member of the League of Women Voters and she'd gotten me interested in the election.

"I think we're missing the point," I said. "It doesn't matter how the candidates spell. What matters is where they stand on the issues. As far as I can tell, none of the candidates really cares about anything except winning. They'll say anything to get people to vote for them."

"My old man's voting for Frimp because he says he'll cut taxes," said Barry Dunn, the class head-banger.

"They *all* say they'll cut taxes," Julia Saks informed him.

"If that's the case, how do you decide who to vote for?" Ms. Rogers asked, obviously hoping to start a class discussion.

Andy raised his hand. "The one who promises to cut taxes the most?"

Just then the door opened and Principal Blanco came in with Amanda Gluck. Principal Blanco is a short, pudgy man who wears dark suits. Amanda's glasses had reddish catsup smudges on them. Josh, Andy, and I shared a nervous look.

The principal focused on Andy. "Did you shoot catsup-tipped straw covers at Amanda?"

"It was an accident," Andy said.

"An accident?" Principal Blanco frowned. "I think you'd better explain, Andy."

"I was aiming at the ceiling," Andy said, then he pointed at Josh. "This fungus brain blew pepper into my face and made me fire prematurely."

"Do you realize that we have to pay the custodians extra to remove all those straw covers from the ceiling?" Principal Blanco asked. "That money could be going to more important things."

Josh raised his hand. "Excuse me, Mr. Blanco, but does that mean that Andy actually *saved* the school money by not firing the straw covers at the ceiling?"

The lines in Principal Blanco's forehead deepened. "Well, yes, I guess it does."

"Way to go!" Josh and Andy gave each other high fives.

"I hate to change the subject," Ms. Rogers said. "But we were in the middle of a debate about the presidential candidates."

"Oh, that reminds me," Principal Blanco said. "I just got a call from the President's press secretary."

"But what about me?" Amanda Gluck asked.

"Clean off your glasses and sit down, Amanda," the principal said.

"But the straw covers?" Amanda gasped.

"Andy saved the school money," Principal Blanco replied. "When was the last time *you* saved the school money?"

Amanda looked very puzzled. She shrugged and sat down.

Principal Blanco turned to the rest of the class. "When President Frimp visits here Monday, he's going to talk to *one* class. And guess which class I've chosen for that honor?"

Josh raised his hand. "Remedial spelling?"

Mr. Blanco smiled. "Very funny, Josh. Actually, he's going to speak to *this* class. That means you're going to be on national television." He turned to Ms. Rogers. "They'll need to prepare questions."

"Oh, believe me, they will!" Our social studies teacher nodded excitedly.

Our principal turned to the class again. "I just have one word of advice for you about Monday. . . ."

"Don't mention tomatoes?" Andy guessed.

Mr. Blanco pointed a finger at him. "Behave."

3

School ended. Josh, Andy, and I decided to meet at my house to brainstorm some tough questions for President Frimp. But first I had to stop at Mr. Dorksen's room. Mr. Dorksen (his real name is Dirksen) is my science teacher and the inventor of the Dirksen Intelligence Transfer System (DITS). The DITS is supposed to transfer learning from one animal to another, but so far it's only made people switch bodies with each other. I once switched bodies with Mr. Dorksen, and another time I switched with Mr. Braun, my gym teacher. And Andy once switched with my dog, Lance.

Since I'd been the "guinea pig" in a couple of Mr. Dorksen's experiments, I sometimes stay after school and help him. Mr. Dorksen is a scrawny man who wears a toupee and contact lenses. He used to dress in brown all the time. But then he married Ms. Rogers and she got him to buy better clothes.

In the science lab, Mr. Dorksen was opening a large cardboard box. Inside it was a reclining chair.

"Is that for your back?" I asked.

Mr. Dorksen looked up. "Oh, hi, Jake. No, this is for the DITS. I'm replacing the animal cages."

"But won't the animals escape?" I asked.

Mr. Dorksen's eyes gleamed with excitement. "I'm not going to experiment on animals anymore, Jake. From now on, I'll be working with human subjects."

"Serious?" I gasped.

"The time has come."

"But what if they switch bodies instead?"

Mr. Dorksen shook his head. "Believe me, Jake, that will never happen again. Since you're here, maybe you could help me move this chair into position. With my bad back I can't do it alone."

I helped Mr. Dorksen move the chair. Another large box stood on the other side of the room. On its side was a picture of a reclining chair.

"Want me to help you move that one, too?" I asked.

"Not now, Jake," Mr. Dorksen said. "Maybe you could come back on Monday at lunch and we'll move it then."

Mr. Dorksen didn't need any more help, so I left. I got home a few minutes before Andy and Josh were due to arrive for our brainstorming session. My sister, Jessica, was in the kitchen, watching the dumb soap opera she tapes every day while she's at school. Lately Jessica had been wearing her long brown hair in a ponytail. She's in the tenth grade and thinks she's hot stuff because she's a good athlete and is involved in the high school government. She thinks middle school is for dweebs.

"Guess who's coming to Burp It Up on Monday?" I asked as I ripped open a box of Strawberry Pop-Tarts. It's really called Burt Itchupt Middle School, but we call it Burp It Up.

"Uh, gee, let me guess." Jessica pressed her finger against her lips and made a dumb face. "I know! President 'I-Can't-Spell-Tomato' Frimp."

I pulled out a Pop-Tart and took a bite. "You heard, huh?"

"Everyone's heard."

"But guess whose social studies class he's coming to?" I asked.

Jessica eyed me suspiciously. "No way."

"Yup." I grinned proudly.

My sister shook her head and sighed. "Of all the luck."

"I'm gonna be on national TV," I said.

"Well, everyone says the quality of TV's gone downhill," my sister replied. "I guess they're right."

I pointed at the TV on the kitchen counter.

"Look who's talking. At least I don't watch soap operas."

Jessica arched an eyebrow. "It's no worse than watching sports."

"It just so happens that watching sports on TV instills good moral values like teamwork and setting goals," I informed her.

"Gee." Jessica crossed her eyes and made a dumb face. "I always thought it was just mindless entertainment."

"Hi, kids." Mom came into the kitchen wearing her work clothes and carrying some big sheets of white cardboard. We were surprised to see her. She works late most nights.

"What are you doing home so early?" Jessica asked.

"I have to make signs for the League of Women Voters," Mom said, gesturing to the cardboard. "For the voting booths on Tuesday. Jake, did you sweep out the garage and vacuum the upstairs like I asked?"

"Not yet."

"Then you'd better get to it," she said.

"I will later," I said. "Right now Andy and Josh are coming over."

"Why?" Mom asked.

"Guess which famous illiterate politician is coming to Jake's class on Monday?" Jessica asked.

Mom's jaw dropped. "President Frimp?" she gasped.

I nodded.

Dingdong. The doorbell rang. "That's Andy and Josh," I said, getting up. "We have to come up with questions to ask President Frimp on Monday" — I grinned at Jessica — "on *national TV.*"

4

On Monday morning I walked over to Andy and Josh's bus stop. They were both dressed neatly, their hair brushed and their shirts tucked in.

"Your parents got to you, too, huh?" I asked.

" *'This is a once-in-a-lifetime experience. You can't meet the President of the United States with messy hair.'* " Josh mimicked his mother's squeaky voice. "How does *she* know it's a once-in-a-lifetime experience? Maybe I'll meet another President someday. Maybe I'll even *be* President someday."

"Not me," said Andy. "I'd rather be a billionaire."

"Or a rock star," I added.

The bus came and we climbed on and sat down.

"By the way," Josh said as we traveled to school. "My father says I should forget asking the President if he clips his nose hairs himself or has someone else do it for him. He says I should ask

14

what he's going to do about corporate layoffs and unemployment in the middle class."

"Is that because he lost his job?" Andy asked.

Josh nodded. His dad had been an executive at a big corporation that had laid off something like 40,000 employees. Mr. Hopka had searched for a new job for nearly three years before settling for one that paid only half as much as he'd earned before.

"You still plan to ask about presidential boogers?" I asked Andy, who wanted to know if presidential boogers were worth more than average citizen boogers.

"Don't know." Andy shrugged. "My brother wants me to ask about the cost of medical care. You still gonna ask what he does if he's in the middle of a speech and suddenly has to use the bathroom?"

"Probably not," I said. "My mother really wants me to ask where he stands on the environment."

We spent the rest of the bus ride arguing about whether it was better to ask about the cost of medical care or presidential boogers. Medical care was probably more important. But if Andy got to ask the President of the United States about his boogers on national TV, he'd be a hero.

"I'd probably get invited on all those late-night TV shows," Andy said as the bus turned onto the road to school. "I'd be famous. The kid who asked the President about his — "

"Whoa!" Josh suddenly pointed out the window. Andy and I swiveled our heads.

"Unbelievable!" Andy gasped.

"Awesome!" I cried.

The school parking lot was jammed with cars and trucks and mobile TV vans with satellite dishes on top. A big crowd of media people milled around while police set up rope barriers to keep gawkers back.

We pulled into the bus circle, and the bus driver opened the door. But before we could get off, a man wearing a dark suit and mirror sunglasses stepped on. A curly white wire snaked out of his jacket collar and into an earpiece in his right ear.

"Everyone remain seated," he commanded. He started to walk slowly down the center aisle, turning his head back and forth as if he were counting us.

"See the pin in his lapel?" Josh whispered to Andy and me. *"He's Secret Service."*

"What's the thing in his ear?" Andy whispered back.

"Earpiece," Josh answered. *"Keeps him connected to all the other Secret Service guys."*

The Secret Service agent walked all the way to the back of the bus, making sure there were no 13-year-old terrorists among us. A moment later we were allowed to get off. Outside, a bunch of reporters with tape recorders crowded around us. "How does it feel to have the President of the

United States come to your school today?"

"I hope they don't feed him school food," said Josh.

"If you could ask the President one question, what would it be?" asked a stocky reporter with dark hair and thick eyebrows.

Josh, Andy, and I glanced at each other. We were too chicken to mention presidential boogers, but the other questions sounded too boring.

Finally I cleared my throat. "I'd like to know where he *really* stands on the issues."

"Wouldn't we all," the stocky reporter muttered.

Briiiiiinnnngggg! The bell rang and we headed toward the school doors. It wouldn't be long before the President arrived.

5

The Secret Service had set up portable metal detectors outside the school doors, and each student had to step through them. Even after we went through the metal detectors they still searched our backpacks to make sure we weren't hiding anything dangerous in our lunch bags.

"Pretty serious security," Andy said in a low voice as we went into our homeroom. In the back of the room, a Secret Service agent was leading a German shepherd around.

"*Bomb-sniffing dog,*" Josh whispered.

In the front of the room Ms. Rogers was talking to two people we'd never seen before. One was a heavyset woman with gray-streaked hair, wearing a gray jacket and skirt and a white blouse. The other was a tall, serious-looking man wearing a dark suit, with a light blue shirt and a red bow tie. His brown hair was neatly slicked back.

"*Let me guess,*" Andy whispered. "*Bomb-sniffing people?*"

"Very funny." Josh smirked.

We sat down and waited for the rest of the class to arrive. Then Ms. Rogers closed the door and introduced her guests.

"Class," she said. "This is Gail Robbins, the President's press secretary. And this is J. Timothy Stone, his chief aide. They're going to brief you on your meeting with the President later."

Gail Robbins smiled warmly at us. J. Timothy Stone crossed his arms and nodded. They both had dark rings under their eyes and looked tired.

Amanda Gluck's hand shot up. "What did you mean by 'later'?"

"The President is campaigning in another part of the state this morning," Gail Robbins answered. "He won't be here until last period."

A couple of kids moaned and groaned about having to wait so long. Then Ms. Robbins told us to relax and not to be nervous when we were on TV with the President. She said all we had to do was act normal. J. Timothy Stone said that when it was time to ask questions we should raise our hands and not shout out.

"Speak slowly and clearly," he told us. "Look at the President when you ask questions and listen to his answers. Don't look at the cameras. And do not ask two-part questions."

Josh raised his hand. "Why not?"

"Because I said so," J. Timothy Stone replied

19

tersely. Josh gave me a look that asked, "*Who does this guy think he is?*"

"President Frimp has been campaigning very hard and is extremely tired," Gail Robbins explained. "Being President is an awfully difficult and time-consuming job. In addition, he's been campaigning for months. At this point it might be hard for him to remember both parts of a two-part question."

"Any harder than spelling tomato?" Andy asked.

J. Timothy Stone's face hardened. He turned to Ms. Rogers. "If this is the way they're going to act, we'll find another class."

"*What a bonehead,*" Andy whispered.

"*What did you expect?*" Josh whispered back. "*He's wearing a bow tie.*"

"I think they were just having a little fun," Gail Robbins said. "Weren't you, class?"

We nodded. At least *she* had a sense of humor.

"Another thing," J. Timothy Stone said. "Don't ask the President any personal questions."

Alex Silver raised his hand. "Not even whether he likes pizza?"

J. Timothy Stone rolled his eyes and turned to Gail Robbins. "I thought this was going to be a class that showed some *intelligence*."

Josh, Andy, and I shared another look. *What a fungus!*

Julia Saks raised her hand. "Why is it bad to

ask the President if he likes pizza?"

J. Timothy Stone started to speak, but Gail Robbins cut him off. "I think it's a fine question."

J. Timothy Stone gave Gail Robbins a stony look.

"I get the feeling they're not exactly best friends," Josh whispered.

"You can't blame her," Andy whispered back. *"The guy's a dipwad."*

"The point is," J. Timothy Stone said to us, "this is the last day of the campaign and we'd like to focus on *relevant* issues."

"But at the same time," added Gail Robbins, "we want to give you the opportunity to ask the kinds of questions that *you* find relevant."

They shared another unfriendly look. Josh and I smiled at each other. This was starting to get interesting.

6

The excitement grew all day. In the halls, the only thing kids talked about was the President's visit. Kids were so distracted that they forgot locker combinations and class times. At lunch I almost forgot to help Mr. Dorksen set up the second reclining chair, but at the last minute I remembered.

Finally it was our last period — social studies. Everyone rushed into Ms. Rogers's room. The desks had been pushed forward to make space in the back for a bunch of TV people who were setting up cameras, lights, and microphones.

"Is he here yet?" kids asked. "Has anyone seen him?" "Where are all the reporters?"

"Take your seats, everyone," Ms. Rogers said. "The President hasn't arrived yet. The reporters are outside waiting for him."

"Why outside?" asked Amanda Gluck.

"Because he's coming by helicopter."

"Way cool!" Andy jumped up and went to the window to look.

"I bet he lands on the roof," said Barry Dunn.

"Or in the bus circle," said Alex Silver.

"Listen up, everyone!" Ms. Rogers got our attention. "I don't want you to forget that tomorrow is your midterm exam."

Andy raised his hand. "But tomorrow's election day. We don't have school."

"This year we do," said Julia Saks.

"Julia's right," added Ms. Rogers. "Due to budget problems, we have to have school on election day."

"Bummer," Barry Dunn groaned, and everyone nodded in agreement.

Meanwhile, Andy pulled open the window. "Hey! I can hear the helicopter!"

We all rushed to the windows. In the distance we could hear a faint *thum-pit-uh-thum-pit-uh* sound. Pressing our hands and faces against the glass, we searched the sky.

"There!" Josh pointed toward the west, where a dot appeared against the clouds and slowly grew larger. Outside, a bunch of Secret Service agents was blocking off the football field with ropes. Reporters and photographers started to crowd behind them.

"Looks like it's gonna land in the football field," Andy announced.

We could see the helicopter clearly now and hear the loud *thum-pit-uh-thum-pit-uh* as it approached. The helicopter was dark green with a white roof. An American flag was painted under the rotor, and we could see the gold-and-blue presidential seal on the door. The chopper slowly settled down on the football field, blowing up a cloud of dirt and leaves.

"Wow! Just like TV!" Barry Dunn gasped.

With the huge blades still turning slowly, Secret Service agents scurried toward the helicopter. A door opened and a ladder unfolded down to the ground. A couple of Secret Service guys came out and then President Frimp himself was standing at the top of the steps.

"It's really him!" Amber Sweeny gasped.

"Who'd you think it would be?" Josh asked.

"I . . . I don't know," Amber admitted. "It's just so hard to believe that he's really *here!*"

We all knew how Amber felt. The President of the United States, one of the most famous people in the world (after our favorite TV and movie personalities, and some athletes and rock stars), was about to set foot on the same football field where we'd had gym the week before!

Inside the classroom, we watched in silence as the President stepped down the ladder and was met by Gail Robbins and J. Timothy Stone. The press secretary and chief aide quickly started talking to him as they walked toward the school. They were accompanied by a group of Secret Service agents, who constantly looked around.

Meanwhile, the photographers snapped pictures and reporters yelled questions. The President stopped several times to chat with reporters, but each time he did, Gail would wait a few moments and then gently ease him again toward the school.

Then one reporter actually stepped over the rope and blocked the President's path to ask a question.

"Whoa!" Andy cried. "That took nerve."

"That's the guy who talked to us this morning when we got off the bus," Josh said.

He was right. It was the stocky reporter with the dark hair and thick eyebrows. Several Secret Service agents quickly pushed him out of the way.

The classroom door opened and the two agents came in and looked around. One held his hand up to his mouth and spoke quietly: *Gateway's clear. Bring in Silver Toad.*"

"Okay, everyone!" Ms. Rogers clasped her hands together with excitement. "Time to get in your seats."

We hurried back to our desks. The door opened again and reporters and photographers began to file into the back of the room.

Then Gail Robbins and J. Timothy Stone came in. We heard a rumble from outside as the helicopter took off.

Three more Secret Service agents came into the room.

And then . . . the President of the United States himself.

7

President Frimp gazed blankly at us. His eyes looked dull. His skin was pale, and his face lined and haggard. His eyes hardly moved. He almost looked . . . like a zombie.

Gail Robbins introduced him to our teacher. When the President shook Ms. Rogers's hand, cameras began to click and strobes flashed. Suddenly President Frimp was smiling and full of life. The room quickly grew hot under the glare of the TV lights.

Gail led the President to a desk at the front of the room and suggested he sit on the edge. Then she turned to the class. "Okay, kids, who's got a question for President Frimp?"

Half a dozen hands rose. Cameras started clicking and whirring again and almost everyone twisted around to see who the photographers were taking pictures of.

"What did I tell you kids about not looking at the cameras?" J. Timothy Stone yelled at us.

27

"Jerk," Andy whispered while everyone spun around and faced front. With the cameras rolling, President Frimp smiled and looked animated as he called on Julia Saks.

"Mr. President," Julia said. "Many people say the social security system will be bankrupt by the time we're grown up. There'll be no money left for us when we retire. What do you plan to do about that?"

"I'm well aware of the problem," President Frimp replied. "That's something your generation won't have to worry about if I'm re-elected."

When Josh asked about unemployment, President Frimp said he intended to look into the matter. When Amber Sweeny asked about the environment, the President promised to enact stronger measures. When Andy asked about medical costs, President Frimp said he planned to do more in that area, too. No matter what the class asked, the President said he planned to do something about it . . . *if* he was re-elected.

Finally I raised my hand.

"Yes, son?" the President called on me.

"With all due respect, sir," I said. "I really appreciate the fact that you say you're going to help fix all these problems. The only thing I don't get is, if you don't plan to raise taxes, where's all the money going to come from?"

"And that's a wrap!" J. Timothy Stone clapped his hands together loudly and stepped in front of

President Frimp, blocking any response he might have made to my question. "Ladies and gentlemen of the media, thank you all for coming out this afternoon. Your next photo op will be tonight at the live debate at the high school."

The TV crews turned off their lights and President Frimp's face went blank and haggard again. Gail Robbins took him by the arm and started to speak quietly to him as she led him toward the door. Since I was sitting near the door, I could hear them.

"How much more of this?" President Frimp grumbled in a worn-out voice.

"Just a few more hours, sir," Gail replied softly. "After tonight's debate it's all over."

"Thank heaven." President Frimp yawned. "Is there some place where I can lie down for a moment and rest?"

"I'll see what we can do." Gail led him out of the room.

And just like that, our meeting with the President of the United States was over.

8

No sooner had the President and all the media people left the room than Amanda Gluck whirled around and glared at me through her thick glasses. "I can't believe you asked that question, Jake."

"Why not?" I said.

"Because it wasn't one they said we could ask."

"Who gives them the right to tell us what we can and can't say?" Josh asked.

"Yeah," agreed Andy. "The First Amendment guarantees freedom of speech for every citizen. That means we can ask the President any question we like."

"What did you think of the answers he gave?" Ms. Rogers asked.

"What answers?" Julia Saks asked back. "All he did was say he'd take care of everything *if* he was re-elected. If that's all you have to say to be President, any bonehead with the intelligence of a Gummi worm could do it."

"You heard what his press secretary said," Amanda pointed out. "He's really exhausted."

"I think you're both right," said Ms. Rogers. "We'll know tomorrow night whether that's enough to get re-elected. In the meantime, don't forget to study for your midterm."

The bell rang and school was over. Josh, Andy, and I started down the hall.

"What a disappointment," Andy muttered.

"Yeah," Josh agreed. "You should have asked the booger question. At least the President couldn't have said he'd work on *that* if he got re-elected."

"And can you believe Ms. Rogers is giving us a *midterm* tomorrow?" Andy asked as we went out the main school doors. "I mean, after the President of the United States comes to your class, wouldn't you expect a night off?"

"Oh, darn!" I stopped walking.

"What's wrong?" Josh asked.

"My backpack with all my books," I said. "I don't know where it is."

"You probably left it in social studies," Andy said.

"I gotta go get it." I turned and headed back into school.

"Want us to wait for you?" Josh called behind me.

"Sure," I yelled back. "I'll only be a minute."

I went down the hall and into the social studies

room. Ms. Rogers was sitting at her desk, reading through some notices.

She looked up. "Forget something, Jake?"

"My backpack," I said as I searched around my desk. It wasn't there.

Ms. Rogers's eyes followed me as I looked around the room. "Can't find it?"

"Guess I must've left it someplace else." I started out of the room.

"Jake?" Ms. Rogers said behind me.

I stopped. "Yes?"

"I'm proud of you for asking that question," she said with a smile. "It took a lot of courage."

"Are you sure it was the right thing to do?" I asked.

"You should always speak your mind, Jake. It's important."

"Uh, okay, thanks." I smiled back. Ms. Rogers was the nicest teacher I'd ever had. Too bad *she* wasn't running for President.

I tried every classroom I could think of. Finally, the only place left was Mr. Dorksen's lab over in the science wing. I wondered if I'd left my backpack there while helping him unpack the other chair during lunch.

Over in the science wing a small group of photographers and reporters was hanging around outside Mr. Dorksen's room. I noticed that one of them was the stocky reporter with the thick eyebrows. The door to the lab was closed and a Secret Service agent was standing guard outside it. I stared up into his reflecting sunglasses.

"Uh, excuse me," I said. "I have to go in there."

The agent shook his head. "Sorry, no one's allowed."

"But I need my books," I said. "I can't do my homework without them."

"You'll have to wait," he said.

"Why?" I asked.

"The President's in there."

"Well, I promise I won't bother him."

"Sorry."

It didn't seem fair. The President had come into *my* room. Why couldn't I go into his? Besides, it wasn't his room, it was Mr. Dorksen's.

"How long will I have to wait?" I asked.

"I can't tell you that," the agent replied.

This wasn't good. Josh and Andy were waiting for me, and I needed my books.

"Look, it'll only take me a second," I said. "I'll just get my books and go. I have homework to do and a midterm exam to study for."

Just then the door to the lab opened and Gail Robbins stepped out, closing it behind her. She looked from the Secret Service agent to me and frowned. "Is something wrong?"

I explained that I needed my books.

"But the President's in there," she said.

"I know," I said. "We've been through all that. My friends are waiting. I have to go home. But I can't go home without my books."

The press secretary studied me for a moment. "You're the one who asked that question, aren't you?"

"So?" I felt myself getting aggravated. "Don't tell me you're not going to let me have my books because I asked a question!"

Now the stocky reporter with the thick eyebrows came over. Gail Robbins tensed visibly at the sight of him.

"Something wrong here?" he asked.

"Yes," I said, remembering what Ms. Rogers advised about speaking my mind. "They won't let me go in and get my — "

"Of course you can get your books." Gail quickly opened the door and guided me in.

9

Mr. Dorksen's lab appeared to be empty except for J. Timothy Stone, the chief aide.

"Well, look who's here." J. Timothy made a face when he saw me. Then he turned to Gail Robbins. "Let me guess. You brought him in because he's got *another* great question."

"He needs his books," Gail replied icily. "He thinks he left them in here. It was easier to let him in than to explain to Perry Sodhander in the hall why the President won't let kids do their homework."

I had to assume that Perry Sodhander was the stocky reporter with the thick eyebrows. At the sound of Sodhander's name, J. Timothy Stone gritted his teeth. "One of these days, I'd like to . . ." he grumbled ominously.

"We live in a democracy, Tim," Gail Robbins said. "Freedom of the press, remember?"

J. Timothy glared at her.

"Anyway, I've got to go down to the office and

get that fax," the press secretary said. She left and I started searching around the lab for my backpack. Suddenly I noticed President Frimp sitting in one of the new reclining chairs Mr. Dorksen had installed in the DITS.

"This feels mighty comfortable," the President said with a yawn. "These teachers sure know how to live."

I probably should have kept my mouth closed, but I didn't. "Actually, it's part of the Dorksen — I mean, Dirksen — Intelligence Transfer System."

J. Timothy Stone scowled. "The what?"

I explained what the DITS was and how it worked. The President's chief aide grinned.

"Let me get this straight." He chuckled. "Your teacher claims he can transfer intelligence from one mouse to another just by pushing a button?"

"That's right," I said.

J. Timothy Stone rolled his eyes. "We sure picked a winner school."

"It's true," I said.

"And what are these chairs for?" J. Timothy pointed to the new reclining chairs. Then he sneered. "Oh, wait, let me guess. Your teacher only works with *really* big mice?"

It was obvious that J. Timothy Stone thought he was the funniest thing since Ren and Stimpy, but I thought he was pretty obnoxious. I explained that from now on Mr. Dorksen would only be working with human subjects.

"Look." President Frimp yawned again. "I don't care what it does or what it's for. All I want to know is, am I safe sitting here and taking a nap?"

"Sure," I said. "As long as no one turns it on."

The words were hardly out of my mouth before the President slipped his hands behind his head and closed his eyes. "Wake me up when it's time to make my concession speech," he mumbled.

I gave J. Timothy Stone a puzzled look.

"Uh, just a little presidential humor," J. Timothy quickly explained. "You wouldn't understand. Why don't you just find your books and go?"

What a jerk, I thought as I hunted for my backpack. In no time, the President was snoring loudly. The guy must've been really bushed.

I found my backpack under the other chair — the one I'd helped Mr. Dorksen install during lunch. I was bending over the chair when the door opened and Gail Robbins came in again, carrying several sheets of paper.

As soon as she saw the President, she froze. "What's he doing in that thing?"

"What's it look like he's doing?" J. Timothy Stone snapped.

"Are you sure it's safe?"

"Actually, it's a major threat to national security, Gail." The chief aide obviously enjoyed taunting her. He pointed at the red button on the DITS. "In fact, do you know what will happen if I push this button?"

Gail shook her head nervously.

"The President will receive the intelligence of a mouse," J. Timothy Stone said. "Which is probably the only chance he has to win the election."

Still bending over the other chair, I grabbed the straps of my backpack.

Whomp! I heard a loud noise, followed by a strong tingling sensation all over my body.

Then everything went black.

10

"Mr. President? Mr. President, can you hear us?" Someone was shaking my shoulder.

I opened my eyes and looked up into the worried faces of Gail Robbins and J. Timothy Stone.

"Oh, thank goodness!" Gail put her hand over her heart and sighed with relief.

"Sir, are you all right?" J. Timothy Stone asked.

I looked down at myself. I was wearing a dark blue suit. I lifted my hands. They were larger and hairier than I remembered. On my left hand was a gold wedding ring. On my right hand was a large gold ring with a blue stone in it.

Oh, no! Not again! That bonehead Stone must've pushed the button!

"Sir, if you'd just say something," J. Timothy Stone asked anxiously. "Something that would indicate that you're all right."

I'd switched bodies with the President of the United States!

"Please, sir, something, anything," J. Timothy Stone stammered.

"Is there a problem?" Gail asked.

"It's obvious, isn't it?" J. Timothy snapped at her. "He's not talking!"

"Maybe he's just resting," Gail said.

"Resting? Didn't you hear what I said before, you dimwit?" J. Timothy cried. "He may have the intelligence of a rodent!"

J. Timothy Stone really made me mad. I was just about to say something when I had a better idea. I lifted my, I mean, the President's hands to my lips and pretended to sniff and nibble like a mouse would.

J. Timothy Stone's jaw dropped.

"Squeak!" I made a mouse sound.

J. Timothy's eyes rolled up into his head.

Thunk! He hit the floor.

11

Gail stared down at J. Timothy Stone sprawled on the floor, and then back at me. She looked shocked.

"Do you think he hurt himself?" I asked.

Gail blinked. Then a smile crept across her lips. "No such luck, Mr. President. I'm just glad *you're* okay."

I had to tell her the truth. "Well, actually I'm not okay."

Gail nodded sympathetically. "You're still exhausted, Mr. President?"

"It's not that," I said. "It's just that I'm not the President."

"I know, you're just a little mouse." Gail winked.

"No, seriously." I sat up in the reclining chair. "I'm not the President of the United States and I'm not a little mouse. My name is Jake Sherman. I'm a student here at Burp It Up Middle School.

I'm the kid who asked the question he wasn't supposed to ask."

Gail patted me on the shoulder and gently pushed me back down into the reclining chair. "Dr. Jeffcoat warned us that the combination of stress and exhaustion could be disorienting. The best thing you can do is sleep, sir. One more debate and then it's all over."

I sat up again. "But I can't debate. You don't understand. I'm not the President."

"Uhhhhh . . ." We were interrupted by a groan.

"Excuse me, sir," Gail said. "I'm afraid J. Timothy has decided to rejoin us."

She bent down toward the chief aide. I got out of the chair and helped.

"Oh, no, Mr. President, it's not necessary," Gail said as she struggled to get J. Timothy to his feet. "I can do it."

"There's no reason I can't help," I said.

Gail stared at me as we got J. Timothy to stand.

"Uh, what happened?" he asked.

"You fainted," Gail informed him.

"Huh?" J. Timothy's eyes widened. Then he quickly turned to me. "Mr. President! Are you okay?"

"Actually, I'm a giant mouse." I wrinkled my, I mean, the President's nose.

J. Timothy stiffened for a second, then relaxed. "You played a *joke* on us?"

"He's still playing a joke," Gail said. "He says he's not the President."

"I'm not," I said.

J. Timothy gave Gail a nervous look. "What's he talking about?"

"I didn't get to tell you this before," I said, "but the Dorksen — I mean, Dirksen — Intelligence Transfer System has never actually transferred any intelligence. The only thing it does is make people switch bodies."

I pointed at Jake, I mean, me, sleeping soundly in the other reclining chair. "You see that kid? Well, he's me."

J. Timothy looked at Jake, I mean, me, and then back at Gail. In an agitated voice, he said, "What's he *talking* about?"

"You heard him," Gail replied calmly. "He says he's not the President. He claims he's a middle school student. But you know what Dr. Jeffcoat said about stress and exhaustion."

J. Timothy turned to me. "Seriously, sir, in a few hours you have to be ready for the final debate. And let me emphasize the word *final*. If you don't put in an absolutely stellar performance tonight you are going to become a former President very quickly."

"Maybe that's what he wants," Gail said.

J. Timothy whirled on her angrily. "What *he* wants? Well, it's not what *I* want, understand?

And it's not what the party wants. So keep your opinions to yourself, okay?"

"Don't talk to her that way," I said.

"Listen to me, Mr. President," J. Timothy Stone said as if he hadn't heard me. "I know you're very tired and weary of this. We all are. But you can't quit now. You have to — "

"Don't tell me what *I* have to do," I said. "*You* have to apologize to Gail."

J. Timothy stepped back in surprise.

"It's okay, Mr. President," Gail said. "We're all under a lot of pressure. Things are going to be said."

"He hasn't said one nice thing to you since you got here," I said. "I don't care if there's pressure or not."

Now it was Gail's turn to step back and study me. "Since when do you care about things like that? This isn't like you, sir."

"I told you, I'm not me." I pointed at Jake, I mean, me, sleeping in the other chair. "I'm him."

Gail and J. Timothy both looked at Jake and then back at me in the President's body. The blood drained out of Gail's face and she began to look a little green.

"I'm starting to feel sick," she mumbled.

12

The spit bubbles really freaked them.

"See?" I said after blowing one up into the air and then sucking it back in. "You think President Frimp could do that?"

J. Timothy and Gail were both slack-jawed.

"I can shoot straw covers out of my nose, too," I said. "Actually, it's my friend Andy's trick. But anyone can do it."

J. Timothy gave Gail a worried look. "Is he kidding us?"

"When was the last time the President kidded you about *anything*?" Gail asked. "When was the last time you even heard him *laugh*?"

"Maybe he's delusional," J. Timothy said. "Or maybe it's some kind of defense mechanism. Maybe he's trying to get out of the debate."

Gail placed her hands on my shoulders and stared intently into my eyes. "We have to stop fooling around, sir. This is incredibly serious. I don't care if you skip the debate tonight. I don't care if you lose the election by a landslide. But you're still the Commander in Chief of this country and you *have* to start acting like him."

I shook my head and pointed at my backpack, which was still lying on the floor.

"Listen," I said. "You've both been with me since I got here, right? There's no way I could know that there's a half-eaten Milky Way in the side pocket of that backpack. Or that the person who had my math textbook before me was Emily Poopert. Or that in my English notebook is the rough draft of a report on a book called *How I Changed My Life*."

J. Timothy went over to the backpack and opened it. He took out the half-eaten Milky Way. He checked to see if Emily Poopert's name came before mine in the math book. He found the book report.

"It's . . . it's all here." He sounded shaken.

Gail turned pale. "How did you know that, sir?"

"I *told* you." Once again I pointed at me, I mean, Jake. "I'm *him*."

Gail's lips began to quiver. "Spell occasion."

"O-C-C-A-S-I-O-N."

"Spell judgment," said J. Timothy.

"J-U-D-G-M-E-N-T."

"Spell Republican."

"R-E-P-U-B-L-I-C-A-N." I frowned. "He can't spell *that*?"

"We've always thought it was a mental block," Gail replied.

"I can't believe this is happening." J. Timothy slumped into a chair and covered his face with his hands. "This is the end. It's all over. Who could have imagined that my political career would end this way?"

Gail continued to stare at me with an uncertain look on her face.

Rap! Rap! Someone knocked on the door.

13

Gail quickly looked at the door. Then she reached up and straightened my tie. "Please, sir, whatever you do, *don't say anything*." She went to the door, opened it slightly, and peeked out. Through the opening I could see the Secret Service agent, and behind him I caught a glimpse of Andy and Josh. They must have come down to see what was taking me so long.

Gail and the agent had a hushed, but urgent, conversation that involved a lot of head shaking on Gail's part. Finally she closed the door and came back toward me.

"For the last time, Mr. President," she begged. "Please tell us you're playing a trick."

"My name is Jake Sherman," I said. "I'm thirteen years old and I live at forty-seven Magnolia Drive in Jeffersonville. My best friends are Josh Hopka and Andy Kent, who are outside in the hall right now looking for me. My favorite foods are pizza, Strawberry Pop-Tarts, and candy corn. I like to play football, basketball, and baseball, and it ticks me off that my sister, Jessica, is better at all of them than I am. My dog, Lance, is a seventy-five-pound yellow Labrador retriever with the brainpower of a garden slug and my mom and dad — "

"Enough." Gail raised her hands as if she couldn't stand another word. She turned to J. Timothy, who was still slumped in the chair with his head in his hands. "Any ideas?"

"Sure, we go to the airport and get a pair of one-way tickets to Siberia, quick." Then he pointed at me. "Better yet, get *him* a one-way ticket to Siberia."

Gail wasn't amused. She started back toward the door. "I'm going to call Dr. Jeffcoat."

"No!" J. Timothy sprang out of the chair and blocked her path. "The media's out there. You're not going to call *anyone!*"

"But he's clearly unstable," Gail protested.

"So?" J. Timothy snapped. "You think he's the first President to lose his grip on reality? They *all* do sooner or later. Listen to me, Gail. The election is tomorrow. All we have to do is lay low until then. Remember, we're not just talking about a presidential election. We're talking about a *national* election. All over the country senators, congressmen, and governors are running for office. We're talking about a *whole* political party! Forget about the President's chances at

49

re-election. If this gets out, it could spell disaster for *dozens* of political careers."

"But — " Gail gasped.

"No buts!" J. Timothy growled. "Don't forget that next January, when a new President is inaugurated, you and I are going to be looking for jobs. Who do you think is going to hire the ex-presidential press secretary who blew her entire party out of the water?"

Gail glanced at me out of the corner of her eye. "He thinks he's thirteen."

"So what else is new?" J. Timothy muttered.

Just then I heard something tap against a window. I turned. Josh and Andy were out there, peeking in! They must have gone out the door at the end of the hall and cut around outside. Andy was pointing at me, I mean, Jake, still asleep in the reclining chair.

"What's — ?" J. Timothy saw them through the window. He yanked open the lab door and barked something at the Secret Service agent in the hall, who instantly spoke into his sleeve.

Uh-oh. I went to the window and pulled it open. Josh and Andy stared at me with shocked expressions.

"Run!" I yelled.

They didn't budge. No doubt they were wondering why the President of the United States was yelling at them.

14

"Listen, you flea-brained, toad-faced mucus balls," I growled at Andy and Josh. "If you don't bail instantly, the Secret Service is gonna nail your butts. Now make like a rain forest and disappear!"

Still looking very puzzled, Andy and Josh backed away from the window.

"Go!" I yelled.

"Hey, you two!" Fifty yards away, two agents were jogging toward them.

Josh and Andy took off. The agents started to run after them. A second later they disappeared around a corner of the building.

I turned from the window and came face-to-face with J. Timothy, who crossed his arms and glared at me. "You're not making this any easier for us, sir."

"You're not making this easy for me, either," I said. "It would be a lot better if you just believed me."

"Look, Tim," Gail said to the chief aide. "Let's be logical about this. Something happened when you pushed the button on that DITS machine. It has completely disoriented the President. Let's call Dr. Jeffcoat. I don't understand why you want to put off the inevitable."

"Nothing's inevitable!" J. Timothy shouted. He stared at the DITS. I could almost see the gears in his mind churning. Then he turned to me. "You said someone at this school built this contraption?"

"Yes, Mr. Dorksen, er, I mean, Dirksen did."

"And he's . . . ?"

"My science teacher."

J. Timothy went back to the door again and whispered something to the Secret Service agent. Then he turned back to us. "They're going to find Dr. Albert Dorkenstein or whoever he is. In the meantime, we still have to prepare for tonight's debate."

"Tim, you're not serious," Gail cautioned him.

"Why not?" J. Timothy asked.

"The President isn't well. You can't possibly put him on national television when he's like this."

J. Timothy turned to me. "You still think your name is Jake Herman?"

"*Sher*man," I corrected him.

"And you're thirteen years old?"

I nodded.

J. Timothy rubbed his chin. "Do you understand that tomorrow is the election?"

"Yes."

"Do you understand that no matter what you think your name and age is, that you are the President of the United States?"

"I understand that I am currently occupying his body," I said, trying to be reasonable.

Gail threw her hands up in a helpless gesture, but J. Timothy ignored her. "Do you understand what will happen if you do not appear at the debate tonight? *Can* you comprehend that it will alter the future of the most powerful country in the world, which in turn will affect the entire world itself? And that this *entire disaster will be all your fault?*"

"Don't you think you're being a little hard on him?" Gail asked.

"I'm just trying to lay out the facts," J. Timothy shot back and continued to address me. "Frankly, sir, I don't care if you think you're Batman, the Three Stooges, and Barney the dinosaur all rolled into one. You have a responsibility to the people and the history of this country. You are their Commander in Chief. You *must* go out there and debate tonight."

I didn't care if my responsibility extended to the *entire universe*. I wasn't debating anyone.

The door opened and a Secret Service agent showed Mr. Dorksen in.

Mr. Dorksen's eyes locked on me. He bit his lip and looked really nervous, like a kid who's been told he's done something bad, but doesn't have a clue as to what he did.

J. Timothy introduced himself and then pointed at the DITS. "I'm told you're the inventor of this machine."

Mr. Dorksen nodded. He stiffened when he noticed Jake asleep in one of the chairs.

"Do you know a student named Jake Sherwin?" J. Timothy asked.

"It's Sher*man*," I corrected him.

Mr. Dorksen's eyes darted from me to Jake to J. Timothy. "Yes, he's a student of mine."

"If someone told you that Jake Sher*man* had used this machine to switch bodies with the President of the United States, what would you do?"

Mr. Dorksen's mouth fell open. He looked again at Jake and then at me.

Then his eyes rolled up into his head.

Thunk!

Another one bit the dust.

15

"**M**aybe it's something in the air," Gail said. She was sitting on the floor, cradling Mr. Dorksen's unconscious head in her lap. I was over at the lab sink, filling a beaker with cold water.

Rap! Rap! Someone knocked on the door.

"*Now* what?" J. Timothy muttered and opened the door. A Secret Service agent came in with Josh, who looked pale with fright.

"Where's the other one?" J. Timothy asked.

"He got away."

"*What!?*" J. Timothy yelled.

"He was faster than us." The agent shrugged.

"I don't believe this!" J. Timothy groaned and rolled his eyes toward the ceiling. "How could you let him get away!?"

"My job is to protect the *President*," the agent said. "Not chase kids. Now what do you want me to do with this one?"

"Just leave him here," J. Timothy said. "You can go."

"No problem." The agent left Josh and pulled the door closed behind him. Josh stared at me and looked scared. I finished filling the beaker with water and kneeled down beside Gail. I pulled up my, I mean, the President's, suit sleeve, dipped my hand in the water, and flicked some spray on Mr. Dorksen's face.

Mr. Dorksen didn't flinch.

"Uh, I think this may call for more drastic measures," I said. Gail understood because she got up and moved away.

Splash! I dumped the beaker on my science teacher's head. His toupee washed off and fell on the floor, where it lay in a puddle looking like wet roadkill.

"Not again! Not again!" Mr. Dorksen sputtered and thrashed around semi-consciously on the floor. "Not Jake and *the President*!"

"Whoa!" Josh gasped and stared at me in amazement.

I straightened the President's sleeve. "Nice suit, huh?"

"Jake?" Josh gasped.

"You can call me President Jake," I said.

"Ohmygosh!" Josh sat down hard in a chair.

J. Timothy cocked his head toward him. "You sound surprised, but not *that* surprised."

"Well, yeah," Josh blurted. "You see, it's happened before."

"Exactly *what* has happened before?" Gail asked.

"Well, Jake's switched bodies," Josh stammered. "He did it once with Mr. Dork — uh, Dirksen and once with Mr. Braun, our gym teacher."

Now it was Gail's turn to sit down hard. "I don't believe this," she groaned. "You mean, the President's *not* delusional?"

"Looks to me like the President's asleep," said Josh, pointing at me, I mean, Jake, in the reclining chair.

"You're telling me that the President's body" — J. Timothy pointed at me — "is actually being inhabited by a thirteen-year-old middle school student?"

Josh nodded. "Sort of like *The Exorcist*, you know?"

J. Timothy pressed his fingers against his temples as if he had a huge headache. "This *can't* be happening."

"I'm afraid it can," said Mr. Dorksen, who was sitting up now and dabbing the water off his face with a handkerchief. "I thought I'd corrected the problem, but apparently I haven't."

"That's it!" Gail gasped. "We can use the machine to switch them back!"

"Can you do it?" J. Timothy asked Mr. Dorksen, who'd just picked up his dripping wet toupee from the floor.

"I'm afraid it might be risky." Mr. Dorksen hesitated and looked nervous. "You see, it's difficult to say what would happen. Switching bodies twice in so short a period could scramble the electro-molecular structure of the individual — "

"Don't give me that scientific garbage!" J. Timothy shouted. "You're going to switch them back, you hear? We're talking about the President of the United States! I don't know what laws you've broken by building this contraption, but believe me, Dr. Dorkenstein, I'm going to make sure they're enforced against you to the fullest extent of the — "

Rap! Rap! Someone knocked on the door.

"Oh, for Pete's sake!" J. Timothy spun around. *"Now* what?"

A Secret Service agent slipped into the lab, closing the door behind him. "Uh, the school principal is outside, along with a woman who claims to be the mother of that boy." He pointed at me, I mean, Jake, sleeping in the reclining chair.

"So?" J. Timothy said.

"They want the boy," the agent said.

"Well, they can't *have* him," J. Timothy

snapped. "At least not yet. Tell them they'll have to wait."

"That's going to be a problem," the agent said. "There are some reporters out there and they're going to want to know why you won't give the boy back."

16

J. Timothy Stone pushed his fingers through his slick dark hair and groaned, "Why me?"

The Secret Service agent cleared his throat. "Uh, they need an answer."

"Go back out there and tell them we need a few minutes more," J. Timothy said.

"I don't think — " the agent began.

"That's right!" J. Timothy yelled. "You *don't* think. You're not *paid* to think. Now do what I told you!"

The agent shot daggers at the President's chief aide with his eyes, but he did what he was told and went back out.

J. Timothy scratched his head, deep in thought.

"It's not going to work, Tim," Gail said. "Perry Sodhander's out there. There's no way we can keep this a secret."

"There *has* to be," J. Timothy insisted, looking at his watch. "Just for another seven hours. All we have to do is get past the eleven o'clock news.

After that, even if the media finds out, it will be too late to affect the election."

"Why can't I see my son?" someone out in the hall asked in a high-pitched and worried voice. *"What does the President want with him? He's just a boy. Would someone please explain this to me?"*

J. Timothy winced. "Sounds like his mother."

I nodded. "Better believe it."

"Does she know that you can, er, switch bodies?" Gail asked.

"No."

"If I let her in, will you promise not to tell her?" J. Timothy asked.

"Please don't, Jake," Mr. Dorksen begged me. He turned to J. Timothy. "I didn't mean to break any laws. Really, I was only trying to come up with a way to educate students without having to expose teachers to them."

"But he's my son. Why can't I see him?" my mother was asking anxiously outside. Another voice chimed in. *"Yeah, what's going on in there anyhow?"*

Gail and J. Timothy locked eyes.

"That's Perry," Gail muttered in a low voice.

J. Timothy took a deep breath and let it out slowly. He straightened his bow tie and smoothed back his hair. Then he turned to the door and pulled it open. Mom looked in with a startled expression on her face. Her eyes stopped on me, then went to Jake, still asleep in the reclining chair.

"Please come in," J. Timothy said with feigned graciousness.

Mom came into the room and hurried toward me, I mean, Jake. Mr. Blanco, Andy, and Perry Sodhander followed her. Andy must have run home in record time and gotten my mother. Then they must have driven back to school and found Principal Blanco.

J. Timothy blocked Perry Sodhander's path. "No press."

"Why not?" Sodhander asked. "What are you trying to hide?"

"Uh, we're not trying to hide anything," Gail said, trying to look calm. "You're welcome to see for yourself."

"Is something wrong with him?" Mom hovered over me, I mean, the President in my body.

"He just fell asleep," J. Timothy replied calmly.

"Can I ask what's going on in here?" Principal Blanco said, looking around at Josh, Mr. Dorksen, and Gail.

"Some unexpected developments with regards to the election," J. Timothy replied. "But everything's under control."

"What unexpected developments?" Perry Sodhander asked, but no one answered him.

Meanwhile, I watched as Andy sidled up to Josh, who whispered something in his ear. Andy's eyes went wide. He stared at me and silently mouthed my name, *"Jake!?"* Without trying to be too obvious, Gail strolled over and started to speak to my friends in a low voice.

Mom and Mr. Blanco were over by the DITS, trying to wake me, I mean, the President in my body.

"Why is he sleeping in the middle of the day?" Mom asked, gently shaking my shoulder.

"I always say these kids stay up too late watching TV," Mr. Blanco complained.

"He does not!" Mom huffed and shook my shoulder some more. "Jake? Jake, hon, wake up."

The President barely opened my eyes and looked up into Mom's face.

"It's okay," Mom said gently. "You fell asleep."

The President, in my body, looked very groggy. "Where am I?"

"You're in the science lab, Jake," Mr. Blanco said.

The President yawned. "Who's Jake?" Then he closed my eyes again.

Mom gave Mr. Blanco an alarmed look. Meanwhile, Perry Sodhander was staring at the DITS. "The Dirksen Intelligence Transfer System?" he read. "What is this thing?"

Gail and J. Timothy shared a desperate look. Somehow the reporter was coming close to figuring out what had happened. J. Timothy must have decided that the best thing to do was get the

President, in my body, out of there fast.

"Let's help him up," he said, sliding his arm through mine and helping me, I mean, the President, out of the reclining chair. I, I mean, the President, looked totally exhausted and still half asleep.

"Is this a dream?" he mumbled.

"Not anymore, hon," Mom said gently. She picked up my backpack and helped J. Timothy lead me, I mean, him, toward the door. "Now let's go home."

"Home?" the President yawned.

"That's right, young man." J. Timothy pulled open the door.

The President swiveled my head toward his chief aide. "J. Timothy?"

"Please, just do what . . . your mother tells you, sir, I mean, *Jake*," J. Timothy replied.

"My mother?" The President, in my body, was so tired he looked like he was sleepwalking.

Mom led him out of the room. At the door, J. Timothy whispered urgently in the Secret Service agent's ear. The agent nodded and quickly spoke into his sleeve. Meanwhile, Josh and Andy started to follow everyone out of the lab.

"Uh, just a minute, boys." J. Timothy held out his arm to stop them.

"But we want to go, too," Josh said.

"I'm afraid not," J. Timothy replied.

"Why not?" Andy asked.

"Would someone like to tell me what's going on?" Perry Sodhander said.

"Why can't we go?" Josh asked.

"Yes," added Principal Blanco. "I'd also like to know why they can't go."

J. Timothy's eyes darted around. I knew what he was thinking: If Josh and Andy got out of the room, the whole world would soon know that their best friend was occupying the President's body.

17

J. Timothy had to think of a reason why Josh and Andy couldn't leave the lab. "Uh, the President and I need to speak to these two young men for a moment," he said, leading Andy and Josh toward me.

"You and the President?" Perry Sodhander looked puzzled. "Can I ask why?"

"Yes, you see," J. Timothy explained, "the President is very interested in what young people think on certain issues, relating to . . . uh . . . "

J. Timothy gave me a desperate look. He needed help.

"Blowing spit bubbles," I said.

"*Spit* bubbles?" Perry Sodhander looked dumbfounded.

J. Timothy brought my friends over to Gail and me. Andy was still staring at me with an astounded look on his face.

"*Is it really you?*" he whispered.

"Believe it, bud."

"Whoa." Andy suddenly shook his head and looked ticked off.

"What's wrong?" Gail whispered.

Andy pointed at me and hissed, "How come *he* gets to be the President? The only thing I ever got to be was his dumb dog."

"I didn't do it on purpose," I whispered.

"Oh, sure." Andy rolled his eyes in a major display of disbelief.

"Listen, barf breath," I grumbled. "You want to be the President? It's fine with me. I'd just as soon be back in my own body."

"That's easy for *you* to say," Andy muttered.

J. Timothy stepped closer. "Uh, excuse me, *Mr. President*, do you think I could interrupt for a second?"

I nodded.

"Thank you, *sir*," J. Timothy said caustically. "I'd just like to remind you that we're dealing with a serious threat to national security here, seeing that the President's body has been invaded by a thirteen-year-old."

"Which, in some respects, means business as usual," Gail quipped.

J. Timothy glowered at her, then glanced out the corner of his eye at Perry Sodhander and Mr. Blanco, who were still waiting near the door. In a hushed, urgent whisper, the chief aide tried to explain the seriousness of the situation to Josh and Andy. If the truth got out, all kinds of terrorists and enemies of the United States might decide that this was a good time to cause trouble.

Andy turned to me. "Anyone gives you a hard time, man, nuke 'em."

Gail went pale as a ghost. "That's really not the approach we'd suggest, Mr. Pres — er, Jake."

"What if something bad *does* happen?" Josh asked.

Gail and J. Timothy gave each other quizzical looks.

"Let's just hope it doesn't," J. Timothy replied. "In the meantime, I've assigned a team of Secret Service agents to keep an eye on the President."

"Which one?" I asked.

"The real one," J. Timothy said.

"What about me?" I asked. "I mean, I may be Jake Sherman, but the rest of the world thinks I'm the President. I need some protection, too."

"I've kept a couple of agents here," J. Timothy explained.

"Just a *couple*?" I repeated unhappily.

"Andy and I are here," Josh added.

"Oh, great," I groaned. "And I suppose you guys are going to throw yourselves in front of me if some nutcase starts shooting?"

My friends glanced at each other nervously.

"Figures." I nodded disgustedly. "The first hint of trouble and you guys'll bail instantly."

"Hey, no fair," Josh protested. "You'd do the same thing."

"Not if *you* were the President," I said.

"You're such a liar, Jake," Andy said.

"Who are you calling a liar?"

"You, jerk face."

Gail rolled her eyes and spoke to J. Timothy. "Excellent debating skills, don't you think? I can just see him on national TV tonight calling his opponents 'jerk face' and 'barf breath.' And I'm sure that threatening to nuke other countries will go over well, too."

"Wait a minute." I pointed at Andy. "That's *his* policy, not mine."

"And what would *you* suggest doing if some unstable country starts acting up?" Andy asked snidely.

"I'd . . . I'd make sure they knew we had nuclear capability and that we weren't afraid to use it," I said. "And I'd use that as a negotiating chip to reach some kind of settlement."

Gail smiled slightly. "I'm not sure President Frimp's answer would have been any more coherent."

"Uh, I'd still like to know what's going on," Perry Sodhander said from across the room.

J. Timothy straightened up. "What's going on is that the President is having a confidential meeting with these young men. I'd appreciate it if you'd leave, Perry. We'll have a statement for you in a few minutes."

"An exclusive?" the reporter asked hopefully.

J. Timothy sighed. "Yes, Perry, it will be all yours."

"Deal." Perry Sodhander grinned and left the room.

J. Timothy turned to Mr. Blanco. "I'd appreciate it if you'd leave, too."

But Mr. Blanco shook his head. "As the principal of this school I have every right to remain here."

J. Timothy turned back to the rest of us.

"I can't believe you're still serious about allowing him to debate tonight," Gail said, pointing at me.

"We'll get to that later," J. Timothy replied, and jerked his thumb toward Mr. Blanco. "Right now we have a problem with Mr. Principal over there. Now listen, Josh and Andy, because of what you know, I'd appreciate it if you'd agree to stick with us for a while. How would you like to be the special guests of the President for the rest of the day?"

Neither Andy nor Josh looked especially excited.

"Are you serious?" J. Timothy asked. "Most people would kill for that opportunity."

"Big deal." Andy shrugged. "It's just Jake in the guy's body."

"Yeah," Josh agreed. "It's not like he's the *real* President of the United States."

"But just think of what you'll get to do," J. Timothy said.

"Like what?" asked Josh.

"Yes, J. Timothy," Gail chimed in with a smile. "Just what *will* they get to do?"

J. Timothy bit his lip for a second, then brightened. "They can ride in the presidential limo!"

"Thrilling," Andy muttered, clearly not impressed.

"It's got TV!" J. Timothy added.

Josh pretended to yawn. "Whoop dee doo!"

"Well, what would *you* like to do?" J. Timothy asked.

Andy and Josh glanced at each other.

"Could we use the sleeve mikes?" Josh asked.

The chief aide shook his head. "Sorry, those have to be available at all times in case of emergency."

"How about shooting some guns?" Andy asked.

J. Timothy gave him a look of pure disbelief. "Get real."

"Could we at least give our friends rides in the limo?" Josh asked.

"And go to McDonald's?" Andy added.

"Drive thru!" Josh gasped.

"Through the moon roof!" Andy exclaimed. They gave each other high fives.

J. Timothy gave Gail a questioning look.

"The presidential limo, full of kids? The drive

thru at McDonald's?" She raised a dubious eyebrow. "I'm sure Perry and his reporter buddies would love that."

J. Timothy sighed and turned to Andy and Josh. "Sorry, boys."

Andy looked at Josh. "Aw, let's bag it. These guys aren't gonna let us have any fun. And we've got a midterm tomorrow."

"Boys, please, *don't go,"* J. Timothy whispered desperately. *"There must be* something *the President has that you'd like."*

Andy rubbed his chin and gazed out the window. Suddenly he lit up. "I know!"

18

Andy dragged Josh off to a corner where they huddled and whispered for a moment. Then they came back.

"We want to fly Marine One," Andy said.

Josh nodded eagerly in agreement.

"Well, uh, it isn't here right now," J. Timothy replied.

"Then get it," said Andy.

"I'm not sure I can." J. Timothy hemmed and hawed.

"Gee, that's too bad." Andy looked at his wristwatch. "Wow, I bet my mom's wondering where I am. I'd better go home. And then I think I'll call the newspaper and tell them my best friend is in the President's body."

"Wait!" J. Timothy gasped. "Okay, look, the First Lady is using Marine One in the southern part of the state this afternoon, but I'm sure later on we can arrange for you boys to have a ride."

"We don't want *a ride*," Josh said.

"We want to *fly* it," added Andy.

"Fly it?" sputtered J. Timothy. "But that's absurd."

Andy turned to Josh. "Know what? Forget the newspaper. I'm going straight to the TV station."

J. Timothy swallowed and loosened his bow tie. "This is blackmail. You kids can't do this."

"Hey, *you're* the one who wants us to hang around when we should be studying for a midterm," Josh reminded him. "Make it worth our while."

"You don't understand," J. Timothy tried to explain. "Marine One isn't just any old helicopter. It's *the President's*. It's chock-full of the latest communications equipment plus all kinds of security and evasive-action devices. It's the most sophisticated helicopter in the world."

"Cool!" Andy and Josh grinned at each other.

"But *nobody* except the pilot is allowed to fly it," J. Timothy insisted.

Andy sighed and waved at our principal across the room. "Hey, Mr. Blanco!"

"Yes, boys?" Mr. Blanco looked up.

"*Okay!*" J. Timothy blurted. "You can fly the stupid helicopter."

Josh and Andy smiled and shared another high five. J. Timothy looked really shaken.

"Did you want me?" Mr. Blanco asked.

"Yeah," said Josh, "we just wanted to tell you

that we're gonna hang out with the President for a while."

Mr. Blanco frowned.

"It's a special treat," J. Timothy tried to explain.

"Well, I think you'd better let your parents know where you'll be," the principal said.

"Count on it," said Andy.

19

We were in the back of the presidential limo, parked in the school parking lot. Josh was on the phone. "Hey, Mom. . . . Yeah, I'm still at school. . . . No, I won't be home for dinner. . . . I'm hanging with the President. . . . No, the President *of the United States* . . . Seriously . . . I'm calling from his limo. . . . What do you mean, you don't believe me? . . . He's sitting right here. . . . I am *not* making this up!"

Josh cupped his hand over the phone. "She doesn't believe me. She says if I don't come home right now, I'm grounded for a month."

J. Timothy took the phone. "Hello, Mrs. Hopka? This is J. Timothy Stone, the President's chief aide. . . . The President *of the United States* . . . Yes, I know it's hard to believe. . . . No, I am not a kidnapper. . . . Your son is perfectly safe. . . . Of course he could come home. . . . The

76

President just wants to spend some time with him. . . . Mrs. Hopka, please!"

J. Timothy put his hand over the phone and looked at Gail. "She doesn't believe me. She says if I don't bring him home right now she's calling the police. Think you could make her understand?"

Gail shook her head. "This is your boondoggle, Tim. Not mine."

"Let's just go over to my house," Josh said. "All she has to do is meet the President and she'll *have* to believe it."

J. Timothy bit his lip and narrowed his eyes as if he were considering it.

"You *can't* be serious," Gail said. "We've only got a skeleton crew of Secret Service. Any side trip by the President has to be approved by the advance team. The route has to be predetermined, swept, and secured, local authorities must be alerted, mailboxes removed, manholes checked. . . ."

J. Timothy smiled. "But that's the beauty of it, Gail. Nobody knows we're coming. We'll pull the flags off the fenders and look like any old plain black limo with tinted windows driving through town. No one will ever suspect who's inside."

"You're taking a terrible risk," Gail warned him.

"Six and a half hours to go," J. Timothy said, checking his watch. "Desperate times call for desperate measures, Gail. Kennedy had the Cuban Missile Crisis. Bush had Desert Storm."

"And we've got the DITS," Gail groaned.

20

On the way to Josh's house, Andy called his parents and went through the same thing. They wouldn't believe he was with the President and threatened to call the police if J. Timothy couldn't prove it. J. Timothy promised I'd be there right after we went to Josh's house.

Gail yawned. "You'll have to pardon me, boys. I've gotten about four hours of sleep in the last three days."

She curled up in a corner of the limo and closed her eyes. Meanwhile, J. Timothy was hunched over the phone in another corner of the car, arguing with someone about why he needed Marine One.

Three TVs lined the back of the driver's seat. As we drove into Andy and Josh's neighborhood, Andy fiddled with one of them. A strange yellow, red, and green image appeared on the screen. It looked like the outline of some land laid out on a grid. In the water around it were small yellow and red dots shaped like warships and submarines.

"Cool, video Battleship." Andy turned up the brightness.

"But where are the controls?" asked Josh.

"Maybe they're in this thing." Andy picked up a silver briefcase and opened it. Inside was a control board that looked like a huge TV remote, only with a lot more buttons. He read down a list of complicated labels next to the buttons. "Let's see now. Under 'Panel Launch Verification' should we go with 'Manual Sync' or 'Auto Strike'?"

"Definitely Manual Sync," Josh said.

Andy flicked a switch. "What's the Sequence Count?"

"Uh, eight, twenty-two, fourteen."

"What's that?" I asked.

"My gym locker combination," Josh said.

"Eight, twenty-two, fourteen." Andy entered the number.

A bright red light began to flash the words, "System Armed."

"Cool!" Andy was just about to press the "Launch" button when J. Timothy grabbed the control board away from him. "Nice going, Ace, you almost started a nuclear war."

Andy's jaw dropped. "You mean, this thing's real?"

J. Timothy nodded. "It's called the Football. It's the President's personal portable communication system to the heads of the Armed Forces, and world leaders."

"Well, excuuuuuse me," Andy huffed. "I thought it was a video game."

J. Timothy made a snotty face. "The President of the United States doesn't have time to play games."

"So which one of these is real TV?" Josh asked, gesturing to the three screens.

J. Timothy pointed to the middle one.

Josh reached down and flicked it on. A picture of a diamond-studded gold bracelet appeared. "Hey, the Home Shopping Network! *That's* what the President watches?"

"He finds it relaxing," J. Timothy explained.

"Well, how do you like that?" Andy smirked. "The President's too busy to play games, but he *does* have time to watch the Home Shopping Network."

"Which house?" asked the limo driver, whose name was Al.

"That one." Josh pointed through the window and Al slowed the limo and turned into the driveway.

J. Timothy leaned toward me. "Okay, listen, *Mr. President*, I don't want you to leave the limo. It's too much of a security risk." He turned to Josh. "Go in and ask your mom to come out."

"Right." Josh got out of the limo.

"When she comes out, you have to act like the

President, understand?" J. Timothy told me.

"You mean, invite her to watch some Home Shopping Network?" Andy asked.

"Very funny," J. Timothy grumbled. "Just smile and let her do the talking. Whatever she says, just agree and promise you'll try to do something. That's what you always do."

"But that's so bogus," I said.

"Of course it is," said J. Timothy, straightening his bow tie. "But the election's tomorrow. Every vote counts."

Josh came back out with his mother. She looked nervous and perplexed as he led her toward the limo. I could read her lips as she asked if this was some kind of joke and Josh assured her it wasn't. When they got close, J. Timothy reached over and brought down the tinted window beside me.

"Oh, my!" Mrs. Hopka brought her hand to her mouth when she saw me. "President Frimp! It's really you!"

"Hello, Mrs. Hopka." I stuck my hand out the window.

Josh's mom shook my, I mean, the President's hand. She looked back at Josh and then at me. "Forgive me for asking this, Mr. President, but what in the world do you want with Josh?"

"Well, uh, ahemmmm." I cleared the President's throat, then explained how I'd visited the middle school that afternoon and was struck by how intelligent Josh and Andy sounded in class.

"There are a lot of issues concerning teens in this country that have been ignored in this campaign. Why, uh, just this afternoon Josh and I spoke at length about the problem of corporate layoffs and unemployment in the middle class."

Josh's mom looked dumbstruck. "Really!?"

"Yes," I said. "I think we have to be more responsible to all parts of the population. With Josh and Andy's help I intend to create the President's Commission on Teenage Attitudes and bring these issues to light."

"But the election's tomorrow," Mrs. Hopka reminded me.

"Well, uh, that still leaves tonight," I replied.

"Oh, you mean the debate," she said.

"Uh, yes, that's exactly what I mean."

Mrs. Hopka gazed at me for a moment. "I have a confession to make, Mr. President. I wasn't going to vote for you tomorrow. But now that I've had the opportunity to speak with you, I think I will."

"I'm delighted to hear that, Mrs. Hopka."

We shook hands again.

"Uh, there's just one thing, Mr. President," Josh's mom said. "It's a school night and I'd still like my son home by eleven."

"You have the presidential word, Mrs. Hopka." I smiled reassuringly.

Josh got back in the limo. As we rode toward Andy's house, I noticed that Gail had awakened from her nap and was studying me with a curious expression.

"What is it?" I asked.

"That was good," she said.

"You mean, with Josh's mom?"

Gail nodded. "You got her to change her vote."

"I didn't do anything," I said.

"Yes, you did," said Gail. "You were *sincere.*"

21

The same thing happened at Andy's house. Andy's father came out and, after he recovered from the shock of finding the President of the United States parked in his driveway, we talked about the rising costs of medical care. Without being asked, he said he was going to change his vote, too.

As we drove away from Andy's house, I noticed that J. Timothy was regarding me in a new light.

"This is interesting," he said.

"It's not a big deal," I said. "I mean, isn't that why the candidates are always out pressing the flesh? The more hands you shake, the more votes you get."

"That's not always the case," J. Timothy said. "Some politicians just have a way with people. They project confidence and trust."

"I did that?" I asked.

"Only because you're not a politician," Gail said.

"So what's the story with the helicopter?" Andy asked J. Timothy.

"Later," the chief aide replied tersely.

Josh opened his backpack. "In the meantime, we might as well study for the test."

"That's right!" I gasped. "We have a midterm tomorrow!"

"Ahem," J. Timothy cleared his throat. "May I remind you that in exactly three hours you're scheduled to debate the other two candidates, *Mr. President*. You'll be appearing before a national audience estimated at more than one hundred and fifty million people in this country and tens of millions more around the world."

"So?"

J. Timothy reached down to the floor of the limo and picked up three heavy ring binders, each the thickness of a medium-size telephone book. "Your briefing books, *sir*."

"My what?"

"Your homework for the next three hours." J. Timothy dropped the ring binders in my lap. "These books outline your position on all the issues that are likely to come up during the debate."

"You can't expect him to learn all that," Gail said.

"Look, he's a smart kid," J. Timothy argued. "He'll absorb as much as he can. If they ask him about something he doesn't know, he'll say he's going to appoint a presidential commission to investigate it. We've already seen how good he is at that."

I picked up the briefing books and dropped them back on J. Timothy's lap. "Sorry. My homework for the next three hours is studying for my history midterm tomorrow."

"Do I have to explain to you again how *an entire political party* and many good politicians are depending on your presence at the debate tonight?" J. Timothy asked, dumping the briefing books in my lap for the second time.

"Well, that may be," I said, dumping them back in *his* lap yet again. "But tomorrow, when I'm in my own body again, I'm gonna have a midterm. And if I don't study, I'm gonna flunk. And if I flunk, I'm dead meat."

"The course of history and the future of this country rests on your shoulders," J. Timothy said ominously.

"That's really not fair," Gail said.

"But it's true," J. Timothy countered.

I glanced at Andy and Josh.

"What happens if you flunk the midterm?" Josh asked.

"I'll probably be grounded for the next two months."

"Given the choice between changing the course of history and not getting grounded," Andy said,

"I'd vote for not getting grounded."

"Exactly." I nodded. "So where's my back-pack?"

Josh and Andy frowned.

"Your mom took it," Gail said.

I leaned forward and tapped on the glass be-tween us and Al the limo driver.

"Yes, Mr. President?"

"Make your next left. Go to the light and make a right. You'll be on Magnolia Drive. Look for number forty-seven."

"Right, sir."

I settled back into my seat.

J. Timothy sat across from me with his arms crossed and a glower on his face. "You have no idea how many people you'll be letting down. Not to mention the fact that if you, as *the President*, come off like a total airhead tonight, it will make a certain press secretary look very, very bad."

I looked at Gail. She was nice. Unlike J. Tim-othy Jerkface, it was obvious that she valued my welfare as much as the President's. When our eyes met I gave her a quizzical look.

She turned away.

That's when I knew that what J. Timothy had said was true.

22

Al pulled the presidential limo up to the curb outside my house. The lights were on inside, and I could see my sister, Jessica, and my mother in the kitchen, preparing dinner. In the limo, no one budged.

"I wonder what's going on in there," Andy said, looking up from his history notes.

"Kind of hard to imagine what the President of the United States, in *your* body, is doing," Josh said.

"Probably freaking out," I answered.

"Just how do you propose to go in there and get your books?" J. Timothy asked me.

He had a good point. It might seem just a *little* weird if the President of the United States knocked on the door and said he needed Jake's backpack. I looked around the limo. "Josh?"

"Yeah?"

"I need you to go into my house. Say you were taking a walk and thought of a question you wanted to ask Jake. Get me, I mean, the President, alone and tell him you need my history book and notes."

Josh screwed up his face. "Do I *have* to?"

"You want me to get grounded for the next two months?"

Josh shrugged. "Frankly, my dear, I don't — "

"Ahem!" Andy cleared his throat. "Hey, goofball, you want to fly Marine One?"

"Oh, okay." Josh reluctantly got out of the limo and went up the front walk. A moment later Jessica answered the door and started to talk to him.

"I want you to think about what you're doing, Jake," J. Timothy said while we waited. "Valuable minutes are slipping away. If you show up at that debate tonight and look stupid, it's going to reflect on our entire country. People all over the world will be watching. You're going to make the United States look very bad."

I glanced at Gail. "Is that true?"

She hesitated, then nodded. "I'm afraid so," she said with a sigh. "Although I still think this whole situation is very unfair to you."

"I never said it was fair," said J. Timothy. "But it's not like we have a lot of other choices. And time is running out."

Instead of going into my house to get my history book, Josh came back to the limo. I rolled down the window.

"Bad news," Josh said. "You're still asleep."

"Couldn't you just say you needed the books?"

"I did, but Jessica wasn't sure if you, I mean, Jake needed them or not."

I turned back to the others. "How am I gonna get my books?"

"Forget about them, *Mr. President*," J. Timothy urged me. "Concentrate on the debate instead."

"And flunk my midterm? Shows how much *you* care."

"Maybe you could study for both," Gail suggested.

"You mean, prepare for the debate? Then debate? *Then* study history *after* that?" I shook my head. "No way. I'll be wiped out."

"Know what would be really funny?" Andy asked with a smile. "If Jake does the debate, you should make President Frimp take the midterm."

The limo went totally silent.

Andy looked around with a surprised expression. "Hey, I was only kidding."

23

But it made perfect sense. "Why not?" I asked J. Timothy.

"Get the President to take a middle school history test?" The chief aide shook his head. "That's ridiculous. And anyway, first thing tomorrow morning we're going to school and switching you back."

I crossed my arms and slumped down in the seat. "Have fun at the debate tonight."

J. Timothy narrowed his eyes at me. "The future of this country depends on you, Jake . . ."

"Get stuffed."

I noticed a faint smile appear on Gail's face, but she covered it with her hand.

"You sure you want Frimp taking the test for you?" Josh asked me. "I mean, the guy can't spell tomato."

"President Frimp studied history in college,"

Gail said. "It's actually a hobby of his."

"Way to go!" Andy grinned.

"This is utterly absurd," J. Timothy grumbled, and checked his wristwatch.

"Those valuable minutes just keep ticking away," I reminded him.

"Ridiculous," the chief aide muttered. "The President taking some kid's history exam . . ."

I caught Gail's eye and she winked.

"He'll never agree," J. Timothy said.

"Maybe you're right," I said. "Maybe I *should* go to the debate."

J. Timothy brightened. "Now you're being reasonable."

"And," I added, holding the President's right index finger just below his right nostril, "on live national TV I could root around for — "

"The presidential booger!" Andy cried.

"The First Booger!" added Josh.

"The *official* booger of the United States!" I said gleefully. "I can see it in the Smithsonian Museum. In a glass case. 'The most significant contribution made by the administration of President Clifton Frimp.' "

"Forget the museum. Why not a monument?" Josh asked eagerly. "Like this huge marble nose and this giant finger and sitting right there on the tip of the finger, like the size of a tank, would be the — "

93

"Enough!" J. Timothy shouted. His face was red and he was breathing hard. "Okay, I can't believe I'm agreeing to this. But we'll talk to the President about taking your test."

24

A few minutes later I was sitting in my living room. Behind me stood Gail, J. Timothy, Josh, and Andy. Mom, Dad, and Jessica were sitting on the couch across from us with their eyes bulging out.

"You see," I was saying, "people under the age of eighteen are not well represented in government."

Mom and Dad nodded dumbly, but Jessica frowned.

"Excuse me for saying this, Mr. President," she said, "but to my knowledge they're not represented at all."

"*Jessica!*" Mom gasped in horror and then quickly turned to me. "I'm terribly sorry, Mr. President, but you know how teenagers are."

"Yes." I nodded. "Among our youth, lack of respect for authority is a growing problem. Of course, if she were *my* daughter I'd see to it that she was punished severely."

Dad gave Jessica a stern look. "I think you'd better go to your room."

"What!?" my sister cried.

"You heard me."

"But — "

"Another word out of you and you'll be grounded for a month," Dad threatened.

"I also think television is a terrible influence on teens," I added. "Especially soap operas."

"And no television!" Dad ordered.

"This is *so* unfair!" Jessica burst into tears and ran out of the room.

The lines in Mom's forehead deepened. "Maybe you were a little hard on her," she told my dad.

"Another area where we've failed is follow-through," I said. "If we're going to be a strong country, we have to stand firm on every issue, from national defense right on down to parental discipline."

Dad crossed his arms and nodded in agreement.

"But I would like to add that watching sports on television is the exception," I said. "It builds good moral fiber. Your son should be encouraged to watch as much sports as he likes."

"Another exception is presidential debates," J. Timothy reminded me, tapping his finger against his watch.

"That's right!" Mom gasped as if she'd forgotten. "The debate is just a few hours away."

"In the interest of time, Mr. President," J. Timothy said, "I think we'd better speak to Jake and then get moving."

"Uh, excuse me for saying this, Mr. President." Mom seemed pretty flustered. "But I still don't understand. Why Jake?"

"During my visit to the middle school today he asked extremely astute and intelligent questions," I replied. "His teacher, Ms. Rogers, informed me that he is a gifted and unusual thinker."

"She *did*?" Mom looked stunned.

"In fact, someday he could be a tremendous asset to this country *if* . . . his life wasn't so cluttered with chores," I added. "He's the kind of boy who needs more time just to think. Give him less to do, Mrs. Sherman, and you will find you have a great mind living under this roof."

"We will, Mr. President." Mom nodded. "I mean, we *won't*. Starting tomorrow, we won't give him any more chores."

"Excellent decision. Now, I think I'd better go talk to him." I started toward my room, along with Josh, Andy, and J. Timothy. As we left the living room I heard my mother turn to Gail and ask, "How does he know where our son's room is?"

"Oh, uh, he's the President of the United States," Gail replied. "You'd be amazed at what he knows."

25

We went into my room and turned on the light. The President, in my body, was lying on my bed, snoring.

"I never snore like that," I said.

"You do now," said Josh.

"Who's going to wake him?" Andy asked.

"I will." J. Timothy bent down and shook my shoulder. "Mr. President?"

My eyelids fluttered slightly. I — I mean he — snorted and rolled onto my side.

J. Timothy shook my shoulder again. "I'm sorry to do this, Mr. President."

President Frimp, in my body, groaned and rolled back toward J. Timothy. He opened my eyes and focused on his chief aide.

"Where am I?" he asked.

"Don't worry, everything's okay," J. Timothy assured him.

The President shifted my eyes away from J. Timothy and focused on me. He blinked. Then he looked down at myself, I mean, him. "Oh, boy," he moaned.

"Don't worry, Mr. President," J. Timothy said. "We've got a plan."

"A plan?" The President sat up and looked at my wristwatch. "What about the debate?"

"You don't have to do it."

"What are you talking about?" President Frimp asked.

J. Timothy pointed at me. "He's going to do it."

The President stared at me again and narrowed my eyes. I thought he was going to get really mad, but then he just smiled. He lay back down and slipped my hands behind my head. "Be my guest."

"But Mr. President, it's not that — " J. Timothy began.

"Can he make my concession speech, too?" the President asked.

"Well, that won't be until tomorrow night, sir."

"So?"

"We were hoping to get you two switched back by then," J. Timothy explained.

"What's the rush?" The President looked at me. "Aren't you enjoying being me?"

"Not particularly," I said.

"Funny, I'm enjoying being *you*." The President rolled my tongue around in my mouth and came up with a spit bubble, which he blew into the air.

"Way to go, Prez," Andy cheered.

President Frimp grinned. "So what's on TV tonight? I mean, besides the debate?"

J. Timothy cleared his throat. "Well, uh, sir, as I was about to say, it's not quite that simple."

"Why not?"

"You've got a midterm to study for."

The President, in my body, scowled. "Huh?"

J. Timothy explained the deal.

The President scratched my head. "So, I've got a history test tomorrow."

"You also have to sweep out the garage and vacuum the upstairs," I added, since he seemed so glad to be me.

"Wait a minute!" J. Timothy sputtered. "That wasn't part of the agreement!"

"Tough noogies," I said.

President Frimp smiled at me in his body. "Pretty sharp negotiating."

"Hey, it's only fair," I said.

But the President shook my head. "Believe me, I've still got the better half of the bargain."

26

We left the President, in my body, at my house where he promised to do my chores and study for my midterm. With all of us in the limo again, J. Timothy told Al the driver to head for the high school. Sitting in back with me, Andy and Josh opened their schoolbooks and started to study again. J. Timothy picked up the briefing books and dumped them on my lap for the last time. "No excuses, start studying."

"But I'm starving," I said. The presidential digestive system was grumbling hungrily.

Andy looked up. "Me, too."

"Me three," chimed in Josh.

"We'll send out for something," J. Timothy snapped. "Now get to work."

Neither Andy, nor Josh, nor I looked down at our books.

"You thinking what I'm thinking?" I asked my friends.

"Believe it." Andy smiled.

27

"Mr. President," Gail said. "I mean, Jake, even I have to protest. *This* is really over-doing it."

"Hey," I smiled. "You only live once."

"But why this?" Gail asked.

"Because . . . the President deserves a break today," I replied with a grin.

The presidential limo was in the drive-thru line at McDonald's.

"But this is not the image President Frimp wishes to present," Gail argued.

"Look, Gail, consider yourself lucky that the President is presenting *any* image at all," I replied.

"It could be worse," Andy said. "We could be out skateboarding."

"Or at the arcade playing video games," Josh added.

Al the driver pulled the limo up to the menu board. I opened the moon roof and stood up.

"May I take your order?" a voice crackled through the speaker.

Josh, Andy, and I ordered quarter-pounders with cheese, large fries, and shakes.

"How about you, Al?" I ducked back in and asked the limo driver.

"Well, if it wouldn't be too much trouble, sir, I'd love the number two value meal," he said.

"Done," I said, then turned to J. Timothy. "How about you?"

"I wouldn't touch that garbage," J. Timothy grumbled.

"Have it your way." I shrugged and turned to Gail. "Hungry?"

"I can't believe this." Gail rolled her eyes.

"Hey, even the President's press secretary's gotta eat," I said.

Gail grinned. "Oh, well, I guess a grilled chicken sandwich and a large coffee wouldn't hurt."

I finished ordering and ducked back into the limo. Al pulled around to the take-out window. A girl in a McDonald's uniform leaned out the window and said, "Thank you for eating at McDonald's. Your total comes to . . . *Yiiiii!*" Her mouth fell open and her eyes bulged when I stood up through the moon roof.

"Something wrong?" I asked.

"You're . . . you're . . . ."

"The President of the United States?" I finished for her. "Without a doubt."

She frowned. "Is this a joke?"

I reached into the limo's bar and pulled out a glass with the gold-and-blue presidential seal. "Check it out."

"Oh, wow!" She turned around and yelled to the rest of the crew. "Hey, guys, it's the President of the United States!"

"That's it!" J. Timothy barked inside the limo. "This is a major breach of security! Al, take evasive action."

"Stop!" I yelled, ducking back down. "Everything's going to be okay, Al. Don't move." I turned to J. Timothy. "You really could have a little more faith. They're just regular kids. It's not like *everybody* wants to get the President."

J. Timothy crossed his arms and slouched down in his seat with a sour look on his face. Meanwhile, a crew of kids wearing McDonald's uniforms crowded around the take-out window holding out napkins and Happy Meal boxes for me to autograph.

"Can I ask you guys some questions?" I asked as I signed stuff.

"Sure, anything."

"You like working here?" I asked.

"It's okay," said one.

"A lot of my friends can't find work *anywhere*," said another. "So I'm glad to have a job."

"Hey!" a kid handed back a napkin I'd signed. "How come this says Jake Sherman?"

"Oops! Sorry about that." I started signing the President's name. "So tell me, what are your concerns about the future?"

The kids frowned. Then a boy said, "Uh, finding a girlfriend?"

Everyone laughed.

"Seriously," I said. "You know what I mean."

"I worry about the environment," said one girl. "I think we're messing it up bad and it's going to get really nasty someday."

"I think you're right," I said. "European countries put high taxes on gasoline use. That could lower the amount of fuel we use and provide money for environmental cleanups."

"I worry about making enough money," said a boy. "I mean, working here is cool for now. But when I want a place of my own and a car and a family, forget about it. I'm gonna have to make some seriously bigger bucks."

"The minimum wage is sort of a joke," I agreed. "Maybe it should be graduated and based on an employee's age."

"I want to be able to go to college," said a third girl. "That's the only way you can get a good job. But my parents can't afford to send me."

"We have to put work-study programs in place to help more people get educated," I said.

Our food was ready, and they handed it through the window to me. The limo started to move, and everyone waved.

"Bye, Mr. President!"

"Bye!" I waved back. "And don't forget, if you're near a TV in a couple of hours, watch the debate!"

Al steered the limo toward the high school. We opened our bags and dug into the quarter-pounders and fries. As that unique McDonald's aroma filled the back of the limo, I started to think about the kind of stuff the President could do. Maybe he really could change the world and make things better. Maybe being President could be kind of cool after all.

Sitting across from me, J. Timothy pointed at the briefing books. "Now that you've had your fun, do you think you might be ready to start preparing for the debate?"

"Hey," I said through a mouthful of fries. "If you paid attention, you'd know I already started."

28

The high school parking lot was filled with trucks. Some had big satellite dishes on their roofs, others towed dishes on trailers. Dozens of vans and limos were parked alongside the school. The walkways were roped off and lined with police. As photographers snapped pictures of us, a group of Secret Service agents led us into the high school library.

In the library, Josh and Andy sat down at a table to study. Gail and I sat down at another with the briefing books. J. Timothy looked at his watch. "All right, *Mr. President*, you now have roughly an hour and a half to prepare for this debate. I'm sorry I can't help you with it, but I've got to coordinate preparation with the aides of your opponents."

"It's okay, Tim." I waved him away. "You've been a big help already."

J. Timothy scowled as if he wasn't sure how to take that. Then he left the room. I looked across the table at Gail, who gave me a wan smile.

"There goes one very unhappy camper," she said.

"Hey, stuff happens." I shrugged.

"True, but it usually doesn't involve the President switching bodies with a thirteen-year-old boy," Gail replied as she opened the first briefing book. "Anyway, there's a lot to go over, so we'd better get started."

We began to review the issues that were likely to come up during the debate. Almost every issue seemed to concern the economy — where the government was going to get money and how they were going to spend it. The briefing books were filled with formulas for figuring deficits, inflation, revenues, economic cycles, and lots of other strange financial gibberish.

Over and over again Gail warned me that I had to be careful.

"You can't say anything that might alienate voters," she said. "You have to tell them that you're going to do the best you can for all of them."

"But so many people want different things," I said. "Anything I say is bound to tick *someone* off."

Andy raised his hand. "I know. Don't say anything at all! It'll be the world's first silent debate."

Gail's wan smile was starting to become a permanent fixture on her face. "While we're on the topic of ticking people off, we might as well talk about the budget deficit."

"The deficit is when the government spends more money than it has, right?" I asked.

"Exactly," Gail said. "It all gets added to the national debt, which is around five trillion dollars."

Josh looked up. "Five *trillion*? Isn't that like five *thousand* billion dollars?"

Gail nodded. "It's a lot of quarter-pounders."

"Even with *cheese*!" Andy added.

"If it's a debt, doesn't that mean it has to be paid back?" I asked.

"Sooner or later," Gail answered. "In the meantime the interest on it has to be paid just like any other loan."

"By who?" I asked.

The press secretary leveled her gaze at us. "You."

"Us?" Andy's jaw dropped.

Josh shoved his hand into his pocket and dropped a dime, seven pennies, and some lint on the table. "This is all I've got."

"I don't think the lint counts," Andy said.

"Don't be in a rush," Gail said. "You'll be paying for it all your life."

"How?" Andy asked.

"It's part of your taxes," Gail explained. "And it's going to grow. At the rate we're currently going, you can expect the debt to reach six trillion dollars in approximately five to ten years."

"And the bigger it gets, the more taxes it takes to pay the interest on it?" Josh asked.

"Right."

"I thought taxes paid for stuff like education and tanks and research," Andy said.

"That's what it used to pay for," said Gail. "Now more and more of it goes to paying the interest on the national debt. That means there's less money for education, health, welfare, scientific and medical research, environmental protections, highway repairs, housing for the poor and elderly, and on and on and on."

"Bummer," I said.

"That's right." Gail nodded. "I hate to say this, but in many respects, the future for your generation, and that of your children, looks considerably less than rosy."

"Like, less money for pizza and comics?" Andy asked.

"Precisely."

"So what am I supposed to say tonight if they ask me about the deficit?" I asked.

Gail pressed her hands together and looked very solemn. "In this case, do what presidents always do — blame those who held office before you."

29

The television lights were bright and hot. Standing on the high school stage, it was hard to see the audience because of the glare. But I could hear them. Reporters, media people, and government types filled the first ten rows of seats. The rest of the auditorium was jammed with "regular" people. Some of them waved small American flags. Others held up signs and banners.

I shared the stage with my two presidential opponents and a panel of famous journalists who asked us questions. The whole thing was moderated by Jensen Peters, the guy you always see on the six o'clock news.

We started the debate with opening statements. I gave the one Gail and I had rehearsed. Jensen Peters had warned the audience not to clap or cheer after the statements, but of course they did anyway.

It was pretty obvious that my, I mean, the

President's, opponents were getting louder applause than I was.

For an hour and a half, I fudged my way through the questions, never really taking a stand on anything that might cost the President votes. I didn't think my opponents did much better, but they always got more cheers and applause anyway. I almost got the feeling that the issues didn't matter.

Then one of the journalists on the panel, a dark-haired lady wearing a bright red dress, asked how we would address the problems we saw in the economy.

I listened to my opponents give their answers. They didn't really say how they would address the problems. Instead they just blamed everything on the current administration.

Then Jensen Peters asked me if I wanted to reply.

Before I answered, I glanced offstage where Gail and J. Timothy were standing. Gail was scribbling something on a clipboard and J. Timothy held up one of the briefing books and pointed at it. I knew he wanted me to talk about the stuff in the book — financial formulas and revenues and interest rates.

Then Gail held up her clipboard with the words "economic cycles" written on it.

I turned and squinted through the glare of the lights out at the high school auditorium. Some of the seats were broken, and paint was peeling off the walls because there was no money left in the budget to fix them. Then I thought about the kids who usually sat in those seats. Suddenly I knew what I wanted to say.

"There are eighty million people in this country under the age of eighteen," I began. "None of them can vote. Politicians talk about all the things they want to do for young people, but the truth is, if they have to choose between taking money away from people who *can* vote or from people who can't, they're going to take it away from those who can't."

I paused to take a sip of water, and glanced at Gail and J. Timothy. Gail was frowning. The President's chief aide was rolling his eyes and shaking his head.

I turned back to the audience. "We keep having budget deficits and the national debt keeps growing. You know who's going to pay for that? All those young people who can't vote, that's who.

"We say we're trying to solve the problems of this country, but the truth is, we're only postponing them until they're not ours anymore. We're just making bigger problems for everyone under the age of eighteen. That's not fair. Someday your children, or your children's children, are gonna be really ticked off when they realize what a mess the people of today left for them."

I took another sip of water. "Today I talked to

kids at a middle school and kids who work at a McDonald's. They're worried about the future. They're worried about the environment and education and getting good jobs. If it was up to them, the politicians would be doing more to make the future better instead of just worrying about getting votes tomorrow."

The crowd clapped a little louder than it had before. Then Jensen Peters said it was time for our closing statements. Since I was the President, I was allowed to go last. I guess that was supposed to be an advantage because most people tend to best remember what is said last.

In their closing statements, my opponents mouthed the same old stuff. They were going to make everything better for everyone without spending any more money. They were gonna *try* to balance the budget and blah, blah, blah.

As I listened I started to realize that it didn't matter what they said. Like J. Timothy Stone said, promise them anything to get their votes.

Then it was time for my closing statements. I knew what Gail wanted me to say. I knew President Frimp was behind in the polls and had gotten less applause at the debate than his opponents. It was pretty obvious he was going to lose in the election tomorrow.

So did it really matter what I said?

"It's time for your closing statement, Mr. President," Jensen Peters said.

The lights glared down at me. I could feel the beads of perspiration on the President's forehead, but the makeup people had warned me not to pat the President's face with a handkerchief because it would rub the makeup off. Heaven forbid the President of the United States should have a *shiny nose* on national TV!

Thinking about noses reminded me of the presidential booger. The time was right. Andy would be proud of me . . .

But I couldn't do it.

Not many people get a chance to be President.

Not many people get to address 150 million viewers at once.

Tomorrow I'd have to switch back to being Jake Sherman.

I'd probably never have an opportunity like this again.

"Mr. President?" Jensen Peters said. "We're waiting."

So why not?

I turned to the camera, cleared the President's throat, and spoke to 150 million people:

"Tonight I said a lot of things to you. My opponents said a lot of things, too. But there was one thing missing . . . and that was the truth."

A hush went through the audience. I heard something clatter. Out of the corner of my eye I could see Gail offstage. The clipboard she was holding had just fallen out of her hands. She looked shocked.

"The truth is that the three of us are here to get your votes," I went on. "And we're going to say whatever we have to say to get them. But by trying to get votes now, we're willing to say things and make promises that will really hurt the future of this country."

Offstage I could hear panicked murmurs and hoarse whispers. Out of the corner of my eye I saw J. Timothy with his hands clenched in fists and his eyes popping.

I took a deep breath and continued. "I have a confession to make. I don't really care *who* you vote for tomorrow. But I do care *what* you vote for. When you vote, vote for the future. Vote for your children and your children's children. It's not fair to dump today's problems on them. So I'm asking all of you . . . please give the future generations of this country a chance."

For the first time that night, the audience was absolutely quiet.

Somehow it didn't surprise me.

Because for the first time that night someone had said something the voters really didn't want to hear.

30

The first person I saw after I left the stage was Gail. She was dabbing her eyes with the sleeve of her jacket. That made me feel bad. I remembered what J. Timothy said about how hard it would be for her to get another job if I blew the debate.

She came close, and I stiffened, wondering if she was going to scream at me or something. But she kissed me on the cheek and said softly, "I wish you really *were* the President!"

"*You idiot!*" someone shouted. I spun around and came face-to-face with J. Timothy. He was red with anger, and clenched and unclenched his fists.

"*Do you have any idea what you've done?*" he screamed. "You've ruined yourself! You've ruined your party! *And worst of all, you've ruined me!*"

He lunged at me, but before he could get close, six Secret Service agents jumped on him and wrestled him to the ground.

One of the agents looked up at me. "What should we do with him, sir?"

"Arrest him and put him into protective custody," I ordered. "He's a menace to society."

The agents yanked J. Timothy to his feet.

"Don't listen to him!" he screamed, pointing at me. *"He's not the President! He's a thirteen-year-old boy who blows spit bubbles and eats at McDonald's!"*

The agents dragged him away.

Then Josh and Andy came up.

"As co-chairmen of the President's Commission on Teenage Attitudes, we've decided that you should remain in the President's body," Josh said.

"But then the guy in Jake's body will be a real dork," I said.

"So what else is new?" Andy asked with a wink.

"Uh, excuse me, Mr. President," Gail said, "but I'm afraid we have a problem. The media is insisting that you meet with them."

I shook my head. "No way. My part of the deal was to do the debate, not hold a press conference."

"But you'll never get out of here," she said.

I grinned. "My sister goes to this school. I know plenty of ways to sneak out."

Ten minutes later we were back in the President's limo, riding away from the high school. Josh, Gail, and I had snuck through the back of the stage and out the cafeteria doors. Andy had gone out and told Al the driver where to meet us.

In the back of the limo, Andy slapped his hands together. "So what's next, Prez?"

I yawned and looked over at Gail.

"The President is supposed to fly back to Washington tonight and conduct a normal day of business tomorrow while waiting for the election results," she said.

"What about Marine One?" Andy asked.

"At night?" I raised a skeptical eyebrow.

"I don't think so," said Gail.

"But you promised!" Andy gasped.

"Actually, J. Timothy promised," Gail reminded him.

"Oh, man!" Andy crossed his arms and pouted. "You politicians are all the same!"

We had to laugh.

31

I couldn't go home that night. Another visit from the President, and my parents would have really freaked. Fortunately, based on earlier orders from J. Timothy, Marine One had returned to the Burp It Up football field. It had sleeping facilities inside, so that's where I spent the night.

The last thing I remember before falling asleep was hearing Gail on the phone, calling Mr. Dorksen, Josh, and Andy to make arrangements for the next day.

When I woke in the morning, the sun was coming up. It was early, but Gail was already having coffee in the helicopter's galley.

"Want some?" she asked.

"Uh, no thanks." I yawned. "I don't drink it."

"Yes, you do."

"Oh, yeah. I forgot."

She poured me a cup.

"What's the plan?" I asked after taking a sip. The stuff wasn't bad.

"With Mr. Dirksen's help, we were able to persuade Ms. Rogers to give you, I mean, the President, the history midterm first thing this morning," Gail said. "In fact, he's probably already taking it. We're lucky Ms. Rogers is married to Mr. Dirksen."

"How'd you get Ms. Rogers to do it?" I asked.

"We told her you, I mean, Jake, would have to leave school early today to meet with the Commission on Teenage Attitudes."

"What about Josh and Andy's helicopter ride?" I asked.

"They should be on their way here right now," Gail replied.

I took another sip of coffee. "Sounds like you've taken care of everything," I said.

"Just about." Gail managed a crooked smile.

"Everything except you, right?"

"Oh, I'll be okay," Gail said. "There are lots of opportunities for former presidential press secretaries. Books, newspaper columns, lobbying — "

"But it won't be the same," I said, pretty much reading her mind.

Gail shrugged. "It's been a once-in-a-lifetime experience. Of course I'll be sorry to see President Frimp lose. Believe it or not, he really is a good man. He always tried his best."

That made me feel bad. "Then I'm sorry I messed it up for him last night."

"It didn't matter," Gail said. "He was behind in the polls anyway."

The helicopter door opened and a Secret Service agent stuck his head in. "The kids are here, Mr. President."

I glanced at Gail, who nodded, and then said, "Send them in."

Andy and Josh climbed into Marine One and looked around with wide eyes.

"Cool!" Andy gasped.

Josh rubbed his hand over the plush seats. "Deluxe accommodations."

A pilot wearing an olive-green flying suit and a helmet climbed down from the cockpit. "You boys ready?"

"Totally!" Andy said.

"Follow me." The pilot climbed back into the cockpit. Andy and Josh went up. I grabbed a handle and started to follow them.

"Uh, Mr. President?" Gail tapped me on the shoulder and shook her head. "You can't go."

"Why not?" I asked.

"Better to be safe than sorry," she replied with a wink.

32

We watched Marine One lift off with a roar and a cloud of leaves and dust.

"Some kids get to have all the fun," I grumbled, only half-serious.

"But not many get to be the President," Gail reminded me.

Near us, a door to the school opened and Mr. Dorksen looked out and waved. "The President's finished with the test. It's time to switch back."

Gail and I followed him back to the lab. President Frimp, in my body, was waiting inside.

"So how'd you do?" I asked.

"On the test? Piece of cake." He smiled confidently.

"You *sure*?" I asked.

"Hey, I'm the President of the United States, right? If I don't know our history, we're *all* in a lot of trouble."

"Come on," Mr. Dorksen said. "We'd better do this before anyone comes in."

He directed us to the DITS and we sat in the reclining chairs.

"It will just take a moment," Mr. Dorksen said, adjusting a few knobs and tapping the keys on the computer console.

"So, uh, how'd it go at home last night?" I asked.

"Fine," President Frimp, in my body, replied. "I did everything I was supposed to do and watched Monday Night Football with your dad. It was a very pleasant evening."

"Uh, great." I was glad he hadn't watched the debate.

"By the way, Jake," the President said from his seat. "I heard about the debate on the news this morning."

"Oh." I braced myelf.

"I'm not mad at you for last night," Frimp said. "In fact, I'm proud of you for taking a stand and speaking out about how you really feel. It's something you don't see politicians do much anymore."

"Even though it means you'll probably lose by a landslide?" I asked.

"I serve the people of this country, Jake," the President replied. "A majority of the voters heard what you said last night. Now it's up to them."

"Here goes!" Mr. Dorksen said.

I shut my eyes and braced myself.

Whomp!

Everything went black.

33
(The Morning After the Election)

"**I** can't believe it!" Jessica shouted as I came into the kitchen for breakfast. Mom and Dad had already left for work. I was back in my old body.

"What?"

My sister held up the local newspaper. A big headline read:

FRIMP EKES OUT VICTORY!

Voters Say Re-election Hinged on Last Minute Appeal!

President Visits Neighborhood McDonald's Just Hours Before Debate!

I felt my jaw drop. "No way!"

"Can you believe it?" Jessica asked.

"I . . . I guess I have to," I stammered.

"I wouldn't have voted for that creep." Jessica shook her head. "Not after what he did to me the other night."

"You shouldn't take it personally," I said.

"How can I *not* take it personally?" Jessica asked. "Mom and Dad say I have to do all *your* chores from now on. I can't watch my soap opera anymore. Of course, *you* can still watch all the sports you want. Boy, if I ever get to see him again I'll — "

Briiiiinnngggg! The phone rang. Jessica angrily yanked it off the hook and barked, "Hello?"

Her eyes widened and her mouth fell open. "Huh? Oh, uh, hi. . . . What!? . . . He's on the line? . . . Jake? . . . He's right here."

Jessica held the phone toward me.

"Who is it?"

"Gail Robbins." Jessica's eyes were wide. "She says President Frimp wants to speak to you."

I took the phone. "Hi, Gail."

"Hi, Jake," Gail said. "Hold on a second."

I heard a click and then the President's voice. "Jake?"

"Hi, Mr. President."

"Gail and I both want to thank you, Jake," President Frimp said. "If it wasn't for you, this couldn't have happened."

"Hey, I just did what any kid would have done," I said.

"Well, you don't know what this means to us and to the country," the President said. "We're going to change some things in the next four years. I think you'll be pleased when you hear about them. And that reminds me, you know the Commission on Teenage Attitudes?"

"Yeah?"

"How would you and your friends really like to be on it?"

"Sounds cool."

"Consider it done," the President said. "And if there's anything else I can do, just ask."

"Well, there is one thing," I said. "I was wondering what happened to J. Timothy."

"Oh, well, frankly, Jake, I don't see him fitting into the future here," President Frimp said.

"What about Gail?" I asked.

"That's a different story," said the President. "As long as I'm around, she'll be here, too."

"Great!"

"So you take care of yourself," the President said. "And if you need anything, you can always reach me through Gail."

"Stay cool, Mr. President."

"You, too, Jake." He hung up.

As I put the receiver back on the hook, I noticed that my sister was staring at me. "Did you just tell the President of the United States to stay cool?"

"Sure, why not?"

She just shook her head and rolled her eyes. "Only you, Jake. Only you."

34

Things pretty much went back to normal after that. At the end of the week Ms. Rogers gave us back our midterms.

"I thought you all did very well," she said as she went up and down the aisles handing back the tests. "Some of you would have done even better, but your spelling left a lot to be desired."

As she said that, she stopped at my desk and handed back my test. On the top was a big red *A-*.

"Every answer was right, Jake," she said. "But I couldn't give you an *A* because of your spelling. How in the world could you misspell 'Washington'?"

"But it's not my fault!" I gasped without thinking.

Ms. Rogers frowned. "Then whose fault is it?"

Out of the corner of my eye, I saw Josh and

Andy with their hands over their mouths, smirking.

All I could do was sigh. "You won't believe me, Ms. Rogers, but this thing goes all the way up to the top."

About the Author

Todd Strasser has written many award-winning novels for young and teenage readers. Among his best-known books are *Help! I'm Trapped in Obedience School* and *Abe Lincoln for Class President!* His most recent project for Scholastic was *Camp Run-a-Muck*, a series about a summer camp where anything can happen.

Todd speaks frequently at schools about the craft of writing and conducts writing workshops for young people. He and his family live outside New York City with their yellow Labrador retriever, Mac.

You can find out more about Todd and his books at http://www.ToddStrasser.com